Attorney-at-Paw

A Chrissy the Shih Tzu Mystery

Diane Wing

Modern History Press

Ann Arbor, MI

Learn more at www.DianeWingAuthor.com

Audiobook editions available at iTunes and Audible.com

Library of Congress Cataloging-in-Publication Data

Names: Wing, Diane, 1959- author.
Title: Attorney-at-paw : a Chrissy the Shih Tzu mystery / by diane Wing.
Description: Ann Arbor, MI : Modern History Press, [2018] | Series: A Chrissy
  the Shih Tzu mysteries ; book 1.
Identifiers: LCCN 2018029880 (print) | LCCN 2018031954 (ebook) | ISBN
  9781615993987 (Kindle, ePub, pdf) | ISBN 9781615993963 (pbk. : alk. paper)
  | ISBN 9781615993970 (hardcover : alk. paper)
Subjects: | GSAFD: Suspense fiction.
Classification: LCC PS3623.I652 (ebook) | LCC PS3623.I652 A88 2018 (print) |
  DDC 813/.6--dc23
LC record available at https://lccn.loc.gov/2018029880

Published by
Modern History Press
5145 Pontiac Trail
Ann Arbor, MI

www.ModernHistoryPress.com
info@ModernHistoryPress.com
tollfree 888-761-6268
fax 734-663-6861

Distributed by Ingram Book Group (USA/CAN/AU), Bertram's Books
(UK/EU)

Readers' Praise for *Attorney-At-Paw*

When Chrissy's daddy is found dead, the little dog is sent off to the animal shelter. Enter Autumn Clarke, a sufferer of PTSD who needs help with panic attacks. Chrissy helps her new mommy and Autumn decides that for her to give Chrissy the help she needs, they need to find out who killed her daddy. Enter Detective Raymond Reed. The three, plus Ray's dog Ace, solve the clues and find the murderer. I was kept guessing until the end, changing my mind several times as to the guilty party. *Attorney-at-Paw* is a fun read and a mind stretcher.

—Carla Jo Worth

Loved it! Dogs do indeed have a way of communicating with us that is hard to believe. The two I live with have lowered my blood pressure so that I don't have to take medication for it any longer. It was a joy to read.

—Cathy Ott

This was a lovely and enjoyable read! Diane Wing's descriptions are so vivid you can easily visualize and feel what is happening. Her characters are multidimensional and relatable. Looking forward to future adventures with Chrissy and Autumn!

—Judy Levin

Diane has created a heartwarming read for sleuths and dog lovers alike. The story underscores that when one door closes, another door often opens without one realizing it. Love is the greatest healer of all pain. After finding and healing each other, Autumn and Chrissy spread love wherever they go while providing healings and even solving a murder. This book is a quick read that holds your attention and resonates long after you have read the last sentence. If you liked the Nancy Drew series, you will LOVE the adventures of Autumn and Chrissy!

—Monique Chapman

Attorney-at-Paw is a mystery with heart. A quick, fun read, filled with warmth and suspense. Stands with anything from the Hallmark Channel. Not just for dog lovers.

—Tim W. Burke

Attorney-at-Paw is a sure bet for those who love dogs and mysteries. While the genre is not one that I usually read, I'm always looking for a book with a canine hero/heroine. Chrissy fits the bill! Looking forward to the next edition of Chrissy's mysteries.

—Steven Cohen

I loved this book!! As I read, I felt the bond between Chrissy and her new pet parent. As a pet parent to a Shih Tzu, Ms. Wing has captured the magic and uncanny intelligence of this breed. I loved the locality to the Philadelphia/Bucks County area. I truly appreciated the omission of foul language and intimate sexual suggestion. This book is an easy read and a perfect introduction to continued writings. Very much looking forward to the next installment!

—Joann Schlindwein

I'm a sucker for a good dog book. Generally, I like to read hardboiled thrillers. But when a good author places a dog on center stage, I can't resist. *Attorney-at-Paw: A Chrissy the Shih Tzu Mystery* is a fun read. I thoroughly enjoyed it. But, what can I say? Who wouldn't like Chrissy?

—Michael Carrier

A fun read: Rin Tin Tin and Lassie would give this murder mystery 4.5 to 5 barks. It's an easy read that starts out a little slow with a great deal of detail as background and foreground. The plot takes several twists and turns as Chrissy communicates hints - in some surprising ways - from her low point of view. Kids 10 and older will enjoy this book. A must read if you, a loved one, or your friend have had to deal with PTSD.

—Charlie (via Amazon)

I love cozy mysteries and this one was a delightful read. Two lonely beings (one human and one adorable canine) are brought together by recent tragedies in their lives. They bond right away and help each other heal by solving a mystery together. The telepathic visions are an unexpected touch. Looking forward to more Autumn & Chrissy mysteries from this author.

—L. M. Spaeth

Chrissy, a Shih Tzu, might be small, but she's protective of her now-dead master. A detective on the scene goes and gets his partner out of the car – Ace, a German Shepherd, who takes over and gets Chrissy to move. Detective Reed would like to keep her, and it was pulling on his heartstrings. Instead, he arranges for her to go to a no-kill shelter. Autumn needed to open herself to love again and heads out to adopt one small dog. As she looked at the dogs, the desperation in their barks reminded her of a fatal accident. One look at Chrissy's dark, sad eyes and Autumn knew she'd be going home with her. A very different type of plot, and very well done. The way the clues are revealed is intriguing. I will look for more by this talented author.

—Ellen Oceanside

This book is dedicated to my miracle puppy, Chrissy;

We helped each other heal after we lost my brother

Also by Diane Wing....

Fiction

Coven: The Scrolls of the Four Winds

Thorne Manor and other bizarre tales

Trips to the Edge

Non-fiction

The True Nature of Tarot: Your Path to Personal Empowerment

The True Nature of Energy: Transforming Anxiety into Tranquility

The Happiness Perspective: Seeing Your Life Differently

Acknowledgments

If you read like I do, you hear the words spoken in your head. As you come across the word "Shih Tzu," please note that it is pronounced *sheedzoo*, rather than the usual mispronunciation using a word that implies poo. In doing so, you'll become part of the movement to correct this long-standing misnomer and celebrated by Shih Tzus worldwide.

I had loads of loving help in crafting this story. I extend special thanks to my neighbor Steve, the pet parent to Chrissy's real-life best friend, the standard poodle, Miki, for our conversations about the book while walking Chrissy and Miki and for coining the phrase "Poodle Doodle."

Thank you to my neighbor, Julie Schultz, pet parent to Chrissy's boyfriend, Teddy the Yorkshire terrier, for her encouragement and inspiration on our walks with the fur babies.

Many thanks to my friend, Ray Eibel, former police K-9 officer, who guided me through likely police behavior with an amateur sleuth, as well as for sharing the experiences of a police K-9 officer and trusted partner, Shep, his German Shepherd Dog.

A world of thanks to my beta readers for their interest in the story and the time they took to provide invaluable feedback that made the book much better: Maxine Ashcraft, Antoinette Brickhaus, Steve C., Ray Eibel, Donna Phillips, Connie Poole, Kathy Sadler, Lauri Smith, and Sue Waddington. Thanks for being an integral part of Chrissy's Mysteries

Prologue

OBITUARY – *The Knollwood News*
Gary Martin – 1978 - 2018
AGE: 40, Knollwood, Pennsylvania

Gary Martin passed away suddenly on Friday, April 18, 2018, at his home in Knollwood, PA. Born in New Hope, PA, Gary was 40 years old (4/20/78 - 4/18/18). Beloved son of Chase and Rebecca Martin and loving brother of Anna Martin. He is also survived by his treasured dog, Chrissy. As an attorney, Gary practiced criminal law in Pennsylvania at the law office of Martin & Evans, LLC.

Relatives and friends are invited to Gary's Life Celebration and viewing on Saturday between 9:30—11 a.m. at Rosencrantz Funeral Home of New Hope, 444 Route 1 North. His Funeral Service will be held at 11 a.m. Entombment will follow at Forest Green Memorial Park. In lieu of flowers, please make a donation in Gary's name to your local animal shelter or national animal welfare organization.

OBITUARY – *The Knollwood News*
Stella Clarke – 1965 – 2018 – AGE: 53
George Clarke – 1966 – 2018 – AGE: 52
Knollwood, Pennsylvania

Stella and George Clarke passed away in a car crash on Tuesday, January 14, 2018, in Knollwood, PA. Both were born and raised in Knollwood, PA, Stella was 53 years old and George was 52 years old. They are survived by their daughter, Autumn Clarke (28 years old). George and Stella were active in the community. Stella did fundraising for the treatment of drug abuse and addiction in Bucks County. George Clarke was a respected CPA with an accounting practice in Knollwood. They were valued members of the community, always ready to help in times of need. Stella and George will be deeply missed by all who knew them.

Relatives and friends are invited to their remembrance on Thursday from 1 pm to 7 pm at Grover Funeral Home of Knollwood, 213 Sycamore Street. In lieu of flowers, please make a donation in Stella and George's name to your local drug addiction treatment center.

Squatting over a dead body was not Detective Raymond Reed's ideal lunchtime activity. The coroner estimated time of death as the night before around seven. It was almost one o'clock now. His stomach growled. The glare from the crystal chandelier hung high over the marble tile of Gary Martin's foyer bothered his eyes and made him cranky. Or maybe it was the fact that there were five officers and medical personnel working the scene and ignoring the little Shih Tzu shivering next to the body.

He stroked the pup's head before going through the dead man's pockets. He found gum, a receipt for the gum from a convenience store with a time and date stamp of yesterday evening at five fourteen, and his cell phone. His keys lay on the floor next to him.

Ray handed the phone to the officer closest to him.

"Sergeant, can you please see if you can find next of kin and put me on with them when you do?"

"Sure thing, Detective."

"Can you also find something to eat and drink for the dog? Maybe distract her with a toy?"

The sergeant nodded and went for the Shih Tzu, who backed up and growled in warning.

"I don't think she's interested, Detective."

Ray went out to his SUV and opened the hatch. His partner, German shepherd dog Ace, jumped out of the back and followed him into the house.

He knelt down next to Ace. "How about helping me with this little one, pal?"

Ace walked over to the Shih Tzu, who looked up at him towering over her. He gave her a little nudge. She held her ground. Ace let out a single bark, and the Shih Tzu stepped away from the body. Ace sat next to her.

Ray patted Ace and his charge on the head and went back to work. There were no apparent bruises or injuries on the body. He looked at the Shih Tzu.

"I wish you could tell me what happened here, little one."

Chrissy stared at him with an intensity that took him off guard.

"The victim's sister, Anna Martin, sir." The sergeant handed over the phone.

"Ms. Martin? This is Detective Raymond Reed of the Knollwood Police Department."

"Yes?" Ray noted her voice was filled with expectation and foreboding.

"I'm sorry to inform you that your brother was found dead in his home about an hour ago."

Ray listened for an emotional reaction but got only silence.

"Ms. Martin?"

"Yes. I'm just shocked at the news."

Ray heard annoyance rather than shock, as though her brother's death was an inconvenience rather than a tragedy.

"Ms. Martin, when was the last time you spoke to your brother?"

"Last week maybe. Why?"

"His dog was found alive sitting next to the body."

"Her name is Chrissy. That dog meant more to him than his own family."

Resentment and cool disgust landed in Ray's trained ear.

"Would you or your family like to come get her and identify the body?"

"I'll identify the body, but I don't want the dog. Send her to a shelter."

Being an animal lover and a dog owner himself, her reaction made him angry.

Controlling his voice, he said, "May we take her bedding and toys to the shelter also?"

"Whatever. I don't want any of that stuff."

Ray clenched his jaw.

"When are you available to come and identify the body?"

"I have to get my parents situated first. It will take about an hour to get there."

"I can meet you at the coroner's office at four this afternoon."

Anna sighed. "Fine." Ray heard a click, and she was gone.

Ray tucked the phone into the breast pocket of his suit jacket and looked at Chrissy.

"Chrissy," he said.

She looked at him.

"I'm sorry little one. We'll have to take you someplace where they'll take good care of you."

Her dark eyes shone with moisture, pulling at Ray's heartstrings.

"You don't want to go with your aunt anyway. Someone nice will come along."

Chrissy put her head down. Ace nuzzled her. Ray asked one of the officers to call Animal Control and instruct them to take Chrissy to a no-kill shelter.

"Can someone please gather all of Chrissy's belongings and put them in bags to go with her?"

He wished he could take her, but he had his hands full with Ace. He watched as a woman from Animal Control gently scooped her up and rubbed her back, while another staffer grabbed two bags of Chrissy's things. Chrissy looked over the woman's shoulder at Ray. When they turned, he saw her tail limp, and almost stopped them, but a strong instinct told him that something good would come out of this.

Back at the station, Ray gobbled a sandwich as he went through the address book of Gary's cell phone. Ace sat under his desk sharing bits of his lunch. Ray methodically made a list of those he wanted to question. Anna was at the top of the list, followed by Gary's partner, Vaughn Evans, and the woman who reported the death, Corinne Taylor.

Preliminary list complete, he called the shelter to make sure Chrissy had arrived and settled in. They reported that she would not eat or play. Ray was not surprised after everything she had been through.

Then he called Gary Martin's law office to find out about his will. A woman named Lisa Coleman answered. She told him the will was in probate and a matter of public record, so she gave him the beneficiary information.

He noted the time and headed over to the medical examiner's office to meet Anna Martin. She was already in the waiting area when Ray arrived, her sour expression contrary to the situation at hand.

"Ms. Martin?"

"Yes."

"I'm Detective Reed. We spoke on the phone."

"Right. Let's get this over with."

Ray showed her into an interview room.

"Where's the body?"

Ray noticed that she did not say "my brother."

"Please have a seat. I'd like to ask some questions that will give me a better picture of Gary."

"What for?"

"Please, Ms. Martin. This is standard procedure and your cooperation is appreciated."

She sat back and crossed her arms.

"May I have your address?"

She gave it to him with a curt tone.

"That's about an hour from here, correct?"

"Yes."

"When was the last time you spoke to Gary?"

"I told you before. It might have been last week."

"What did you talk about?"

"What we always talk about. I needed money to take care of my parents."

"Did Gary provide for them normally?"

"Not voluntarily. I always had to ask. Listen, I need to get back home."

"We're almost finished. How would you describe your relationship with the deceased?"

She chuckled. "Not great. We only spoke when we had to. Now I don't need to speak with him at all." Her mouth tightened to a thin line.

"Where were you day before yesterday around seven in the evening?"

"Home with my parents." She said without hesitation.

Ray nodded his head and made a note.

"Were you aware that you are the sole beneficiary in Mr. Martin's will?"

"Does that make me some kind of suspect?"

"What do you believe Mr. Martin died from?"

"How should I know? I'm not a doctor!" She waited a beat. "That's enough. Show me the body and let me get out of here."

Ray closed his notepad and showed her into the viewing room.

∽

Autumn Clarke shook off visions of the tractor-trailer grill filling the windshield and echoes of twisting metal, screams, and sirens. Toes curling in her shoes, she steadied herself against the brick wall and took a calming, deep breath that brought her back to the present. She looked around to see if anyone witnessed her episode. She hated when it happened in public places and desperately wanted to reclaim her self-control.

Panic subsiding, her focus shifted to the industrial glass doors that challenged her to enter with no promise of success. Autumn was afraid to love again, yet embers of hope glowed in the darkness and faith smoldered in her heart. This was the first step toward healing, and she opened to it like a folklorist drawn to an ancient fairy tale.

Her treatment plan had hit a wall. The nightmares of that fateful day crept into her waking consciousness. The recent rise in anxiety prompted her psychiatrist, Doctor Wesley Harper, to add this latest intervention. To heal, she needed to welcome love back into her life. So here she stood, despite intense skepticism and fear.

Taking a deep breath, she took a leap of faith with nothing to lose. She pulled open the glass door to the sterile, cinder block building, the smell of pungent disinfectant conjuring images of the hospital emergency room. Chest tight and tears glistening, she defied the urge to leave. The heels of her scuffed brown leather booties pounded the black and white tile floor and echoed off the bare walls up to the receptionist desk. The noise gave her courage somehow; it sounded strong and purposeful.

The wood-look laminate receptionist desk felt cold, yet the carrot-topped, curly-haired receptionist with the bright, friendly smile warmed the space. Her official clip-on tag revealed her name as Brenda.

"May I help you?"

Brenda wore a bright yellow T-shirt emblazoned with an illustration of a small, furry dog of no particular breed wearing a halo and the call to action: *Adopt a Fuzzy Angel Today.*

"Hi Brenda, I'm here to adopt a fuzzy angel."

Autumn and Brenda shared a smile, and Autumn's tension subsided.

"I'm happy to help you with that."

"I'm Autumn Clarke. I filled out the adoption application form on your website. Six pages' worth."

"We want to be sure that our fur babies go to the best homes," Brenda said as she typed Autumn's name into the computer system. "Here you are. Yes, your application is approved."

"I'd like a small breed, under 20 pounds."

"Wonderful! The sweetest little girl came in this afternoon. Right this way. She's a Shih Tzu."

Brenda led her down a drab, narrow hallway, wide hips swaying under the form-fitting T-shirt, and into the caged area. It was depressing to see these beautiful furry faces staring with soulful eyes from behind bars. Autumn wondered how big a heart was required to work here and stay strong. The stories she read on the shelter's website of how they got here were as sad as their expressions. They reminded Autumn of herself, caged by the memory of a fatal accident that haunted her day and night.

Their desperation, and her own, bounced off the walls and echoed back like a lonely coyote's cry in a canyon. Some dogs barked with loud and frantic tones. Others kept to themselves, withdrawn in uncertainty for the future. Autumn tried not to think about it and to focus on the one she was here to see.

Having a pet had never occurred to her. In all of the wonderful experiences her parents had brought her, none included a pet of any kind.

7

Not even a fish. So, now to be responsible for the wellbeing of a dog made her hands go clammy and her heart race.

The idea of entering into a relationship seemed foreign. The *Land of Connection* was a place she had visited long ago and could only recall pieces of the trip. She was afraid of attachment. She worried that her treatment plan would not work. She dreaded being alone forever. Despite intense skepticism and fear, to heal, she needed to welcome love back into her life.

Her personal default was to research whatever challenge she faced or topic she wrote about as a freelance journalist. She'd spent several evenings poring over the massive amount of information online about what it is like to have a dog before following her doctor's suggestion and making the decision to adopt. She learned what a huge undertaking it is to have a pet; her choice to show up anyway demonstrating the commitment to her healing and improving the life of a little dog in the process.

Still, her stomach tightened at the thought of having an animal in the house. She used Dr. Wes' trick of feeling her feet on the floor and focusing her attention on Brenda, noting every movement she made to keep her mind occupied. His methods were effective, albeit non-traditional at times. That was what she liked most about him. The latest suggestion forced her to step out of her comfort zone and tackle this latest challenge.

"Here she is." Brenda petted the little dog through the bars.

The moment the Shih Tzu lifted her angelic face and stared straight into Autumn Clarke's eyes, she knew this little cutie was coming home with her. The sad, dark eyes looked at Autumn through tangled white bangs. The one stuffed toy in her cage went ignored. This little dog reflected Autumn's own sorrow and loss of hope.

Dr. Wes's idea to get an emotional support dog as complementary treatment might work out after all. A glimmer of hope sparkled in the dark place that had become her world, for herself and for this precious treasure.

"Her name is Chrissy. She's three years old," said Brenda. Chrissy gave the softest wave of her tail, and Autumn stuck her fingers through the bars of the cage. Chrissy sniffed and then nuzzled Autumn's hand. The dog was white and charcoal gray with a tuft of white like a halo over her forehead.

"She's so adorable. How did she end up here?"

"Her pet parent died yesterday," Brenda said. "He lived alone and Chrissy sat next to his body overnight, until a friend found them and called 911."

Autumn gasped.

"How did he die?"

"From what I hear, a heart attack."

She connected with Chrissy's circumstances, her own parents lost to her in a sudden, tragic accident three months earlier. Autumn was the only survivor. She leaned closer and whispered, "Poor baby!" Chrissy blissfully closed her eyes and pressed into Autumn's fingers. For the first time since the accident, Autumn felt warmth in the spot where her heart had ached with cold. Maybe Dr. Wes was right. Maybe she and Chrissy could help each other.

"I'm surprised no one took her in."

"The family had no interest in taking her, so animal control brought her to us."

Chrissy now paid attention, her eyes alert, seeming to know they were talking about her.

Brenda continued, "You should know that Shih Tzus were bred as companion animals, so they are affectionate lap-dogs who love to be loved and to give love. Because of that, this breed is prone to separation anxiety, and her recent experience exacerbated that, so she has severe separation anxiety. I've been spending as much time with her as I can since she came in. She shakes uncontrollably when left alone."

"Who doesn't," mumbled Autumn.

"Excuse me?"

"Nothing."

"Are you still interested? Most people don't want to deal with that kind of issue."

"I don't mind. I work from home, so there's no need for us to be separated."

Autumn didn't let Brenda know that Chrissy was destined to be an emotional support animal, able to accompany her everywhere. It was embarrassing to show weakness, especially to strangers. Her father had taught her to be strong, and part of her felt guilty for dropping the ball on that lesson.

Brenda opened the cage door. The button nose surrounded by long, white hair captured Autumn, the joy and affection expressed in a broad smile she had lost along with her parents. Chrissy was cuter than a stuffed animal, her intent stare of anticipation emanating from her white and gray face.

Autumn reached in and pulled Chrissy out, cuddling her against her chest. Chrissy rested her head on Autumn's shoulder, sorrow and relief pouring from her small body in little tremors. She gave her a loving squeeze and stroked her head. Chrissy grunted and sighed. Thinking about helping this little girl opened Autumn's heart and filled it with tenderness.

"She's perfect," she said to Brenda, and then to Chrissy, "Want to come home with me?"

Chrissy cooed on cue, and snuggled against Autumn.

Autumn closed her eyes, savoring the delightful feeling of Chrissy's head, so trusting against her neck. "Where do I sign?"

A half hour later, Autumn strolled out of the shelter with her new furry friend and two kitchen-sized trash bags full of everything a well-cared-for Shih Tzu needs: clothes, lots of toys, two doggie beds, harnesses, bowls, leashes, brushes, and bows gathered from her former home by the police.

"Boy, your daddy loved you! You have so many nice things."

Chrissy looked up at Autumn, acknowledging the truth of this statement, a hint of a smile on Chrissy's little black lips.

Autumn lifted her onto the soft, pink blanket covering the pristine beige leather backseat of the silver Mercedes SUV. Chrissy cooperated and settled onto the blanket, her tail wrapped around the side of her body. Autumn petted her head and closed the car door. She opened the hatch and threw the bags into the back.

The Mercedes was part of Autumn's inheritance and kept her parents close to her. She and her mother had food-shopped in it and took trips to the mall, loading the spacious back with their finds. Riding in it soothed the persistent anxiety marking Autumn's life since the death of her parents, Stella and George Clarke.

Her parents had been the biggest part of her world. She shared with them joys, sorrows, successes, and missteps; all experiences met with equal attention and trusted counsel. In her twenty-eight years of life, they were never too busy to listen or to share the major and minor moments of Autumn's life. She accompanied them to charitable events and to dinner parties. Friends were welcomed with open arms, and gatherings were celebrations of love and life. Their home was happy and peaceful in general, with rare times of angst.

Autumn glanced at her new charge curled up on the blanket, her heart fluttering. She smiled when Chrissy lifted her head to gaze back at her with a slight tilt of her head. She reached between the seats and scratched Chrissy's ears, and then pulled the seatbelt across her chest.

Autumn checked her rearview mirrors and inched out of the parking space. A red flash alerted her to the fast approach of a car. Autumn's foot stomped the brake, jarring Chrissy in the backseat. She flung her hand to steady the little body and watched the car zoom past.

Autumn's breath caught, along with her seatbelt. The seatbelt tightened in the same way as when the tractor-trailer had slammed head-on into her parents' Audi, killing them both and sparing Autumn, who was riding in the backseat. The sensation settled in, triggering hyperventilation and paralysis. She heard Chrissy growling in the distance. Face numb, she fought to refocus on the present, but the memories persisted.

They had been on their way to a fundraiser supporting her mother's work with an organization addressing drug abuse and addiction in Bucks County. The opioid-filled truck driver who had lost control of the truck proved the need for the foundation.

Chrissy's growls turned to insistent barks, bringing Autumn back from the shadows of the past. She reached back and gave Chrissy a loving squeeze.

"What a smart girl! I'm okay now, sweetheart."

Chrissy grunted and sighed.

Autumn took a few deep breaths to regroup.

"Let's go shopping!"

Taking another long, cautious look around the parking lot, Autumn pulled out and headed to the local pet superstore.

Chrissy perked up as they entered through the sliding automatic doors. Everyone who passed her smiled or reached out to pet her. She reveled in the attention, giving a wag when people made a fuss. Chrissy walked over to the freezer section, sat down in front of the shelf, and looked at Autumn.

"Really? You know what type of food this is?"

Chrissy beat her tail against the floor and licked her lips. Autumn held up various food choices until Chrissy gave a single bark indicating the one she wanted. They did the same with snacks and toys. Chrissy chose a small, blue ball and a bright pink stuffed piggy with a squeaker inside. Autumn shook her head, watching the way Chrissy made decisions. It was endearing and a little eerie at the same time.

Thinking of the sudden stop she had made in the rescue shelter parking lot, she bought the most secure, comfortable pet seat they had. The red lining with tan outer material coordinated with the beige interior of the Mercedes.

At the car, Autumn removed the pet safety seat from the bag and put the rest of Chrissy's things in the hatchback. She reached down to put Chrissy in the front seat while she dealt with installing Chrissy's new perch. It only took a few minutes to set up, line it with the pink blanket, and plop Chrissy in.

"There, safe and sound. Comfy?"

Chrissy made a little snorting sound. Autumn shook her head and caressed Chrissy's face in adoration. She wondered if all dogs were this aware.

With both hands on the wheel to ensure ultimate control of the vehicle, she drove the short distance through light traffic on the main roads, past the Giant supermarket and the medical center and onto the peaceful, tree-lined street of Acorn Lane. Dappled sunlight permeated the canopy of green that shaded pedestrians, drivers, and kids on bikes.

She drove past well-kept lawns and box-shaped Japanese holly bushes that filled her mind with happy childhood memories. Her family's Bucks County farmhouse made of Pennsylvania fieldstone and wood sat on almost two acres of land. The privacy it afforded was one of her mother's favorite aspects of the house, while Dad liked the solid warmth of the stone and plaster. His favorite comment about the house, "They don't build them like this anymore," echoed in Autumn's mind.

The divided light windows and doors, painted weathered navy blue, brought out the nineteenth century elements of the building. The home renovation was a labor of love her parents had undertaken in detail, keeping the historic ornamentation while modernizing the electric, plumbing, and kitchen. It was comfortable and inspiring, her imagination sparked by the Nancy Drew books she had read as a child sitting in the window seat of the library room. Fond memories of her parents lingered reading her stories aloud and encouraging her to write and her outdoor adventures in the neighborhood.

The house and everything in it belonged to her now. Despite her financial wealth, she would rather have her parents than their things.

She took a deep breath and clicked the garage door opener. She looked at Chrissy to see if she reacted to the noise of the motor. Chrissy was perfectly calm and met Autumn's eyes, telling her she was fine with it.

Now I'm thinking this dog can tell me things. Am I not crazy enough as it is?

Autumn rolled the car into her mother's side of the two-car garage. The windshield hit the tennis ball hanging from the ceiling, and she closed the door behind them. Dad had installed this safeguard after Mom overshot the length of the garage and scraped the front bumper while causing a dent in the garage wall and Mom's ego. They teased her about it whenever possible. The dent remained, and tore at the nick in her heart each time she saw it. She thought about getting it fixed but the thought of doing so threatened to erase a part of the relationship she had with her parents.

Her own bluish-silver Prius sat parked in her father's spot. The insurance company totaled the twisted heap of metal that was his Audi after the accident.

Thoughts of her dad pulling into the garage after a long day at his thriving accounting firm flooded her mind. George Clarke taught his daughter to be strong, to have a will, and to persist when the going got tough. She had let him down. Hands gripping the wheel, she sat there, silent tears flowing down her cheeks. She whispered "Miss you," and grabbed a tissue from the ever-present box next to her. Another deep breath and she stepped out of the car.

She lifted Chrissy from her car seat and put her on the floor, removing the leash and guiding her through the entry door into the laundry room adjacent to a kitchen any chef would enjoy. Her mother, Stella, loved to cook, and the six-burner Viking stove, pale maple cabinets, and travertine backsplash reflected quality design and a love of feeding her family.

Stella flourished in her domestic role, happy to sew, clean, and cook, while running successful fund raising events for The Advocates of Southeast Pennsylvania, a group dedicated to prevention, intervention, and addiction recovery solutions. Her mother's interest in this particular nonprofit rose from losing her cousin to opioid addiction.

Chrissy sniffed the doorframe and the floor before padding into the kitchen of her new home. Autumn followed with the bags of goodies from the pet store and the shelter. She washed Chrissy's bowls, filled one with filtered water, and placed them on the floor on a cloth placemat bordered with flowers. Chrissy drank with gusto, lifted her dripping chin, and looked at Autumn with thanks, her black lips curving into a smile. She ambled over to the sliding glass doors that led to a patio and fenced yard.

"Outside? Glad you're housetrained."

Autumn slid open the door and Chrissy stepped across the threshold. She sat on the patio and checked out her new, fenced yard and lush green surroundings. She walked over to the thick lawn, relieved herself, and then came right back to Autumn. Never having had a dog before, she did not know quite what to expect, and wondered if this was normal. Were all dogs this cooperative and laid-back? Did they all have the ability to convey exactly what they wanted? If not, she had certainly lucked out in finding Chrissy.

Autumn grabbed an iced tea and she and Chrissy sat outside together. The late spring afternoon was sunny and pleasant, birds chirping and squirrels scampering in the yard. This was Stella Clarke's favorite time of year, anticipating the cycle of blossoms that added seasonal beauty to the garden. Autumn petted Chrissy, who accepted the attention and pushed her head against her hand. She looked up at Autumn with watery eyes that were deeper than any human's she'd ever encountered.

"You miss your daddy?"

Chrissy stared back in response.

"I know. I miss mine, too."

They understood each other's pain. Autumn picked up her new friend and snuggled her between her outstretched legs so she could see the birds and squirrels enjoying the leafing sycamore and maple trees. Chrissy settled in, the sun and the warm spring breeze gently touching Autumn's skin and ruffling Chrissy's hair. Autumn's body released tension for the first time since losing her parents. Chrissy let out a deep sigh. They both closed their eyes and took a much-needed nap.

≠ 2 ≠

Refreshed from their nap, they headed into the kitchen.

"You must be hungry."

Autumn sensed Chrissy's eyes on her as she moved about the neat and efficient kitchen. She held up a bag of food. Chrissy made no indication of being excited about her meal. Autumn scooped some raw food into the bowl and let it thaw for a couple of minutes according to the package directions. Chrissy watched as she placed the bowl on the placemat, but made no move to eat.

"What's the matter, baby?"

Chrissy looked at her. Autumn dug out a piece of meat from the bowl and held it up.

"Look how good this is!" She pretended to eat it.

Chrissy took a few steps toward the food and stopped when Autumn put the meat back into the bowl. Autumn pulled it back out and offered it to her, this time waiting until she was close enough to take it from Autumn's fingers. She gently took the morsel, chewed it in two bites, and swallowed, licking her lips. Autumn sat on the floor next to Chrissy's bowl and urged her toward the meal piece by piece, until finally Chrissy decided it was okay to eat it by herself. She finished off with a drink of water and looked at Autumn.

"Good girl!"

Chrissy gave a half-hearted wag of her tail.

Autumn took her evening dose of medication while making her own dinner of salmon and roasted asparagus. Chrissy showed no interest. She had heard stories of dogs begging and wanting to eat everything in sight. This one had to be encouraged to eat beef.

Chrissy sat under the kitchen table with no sound or movement as Autumn ate, watching the television her father had installed over the counter. He was handy around the house, and her mother always made a fuss over him when he finished a project. God, she missed them.

Her breath became ragged and suddenly Chrissy was next to her making a low, growling sound. Autumn looked at the angelic face and her breath normalized. She took a deep breath and focused her attention on Chrissy. This little girl was a natural therapist. Autumn calmed and sensed Chrissy's need to go outside.

"Let's go for a walk!"

Chrissy stood alert at the word "walk," and moseyed to the front door. Autumn grabbed the harness and leash and secured her before opening the door. Nose to the ground, Chrissy explored the smells of her new neighborhood. She chose a spot on the lawn and squatted.

"What a good girl!"

Tail wagging at the compliment, Chrissy decided to turn right when they reached the sidewalk. Twilight closed in on them and reminded Autumn of the moment the emergency medical technician broke the news that her parents did not survive the crash. A lump rose in her throat, tears building. With the dimming light, it would be harder for her neighbors to see her sorrow. A little tug in her hand pulled her attention toward Chrissy doing her business on a patch of grass next to the street. The memory faded as Autumn's thoughts shifted to what Chrissy was doing while she got a poo bag ready.

"You're such a dear blessing."

Chrissy finished and they continued walking down the street enjoying the warm spring evening and the honeysuckle-perfumed air as they walked. A neighbor came out of his front door, white standard poodle in tow. Autumn had never before noticed when people walked their dogs. Now she was one of them.

"Hey, Steve!" Autumn called.

Her longtime neighbor, Steve Coleman, stopped and waited for them to catch up. His slender frame and graying hair reminded her of her father. He looked comfortable in his thick cotton T-shirt and cargo shorts. Autumn reached out to pet the poodle.

"Hi, Mickey!"

Chrissy approached Mickey and sniffed him. He towered over her but was gentle in his olfactory assessment of his new friend. They both wagged their tails.

"A new addition!"

"This is Chrissy."

Steve reached down and petted Chrissy enthusiastically. She allowed it.

"Hello, Chrissy. Looks like they're going to be friends. Want to join us? We're going around the block."

"Sure!"

It was nice to have some human company as well as Chrissy. Autumn noticed Steve's strained, careful gait from his recent back and neck surgery and slowed to match his speed. He had heart and blood pressure issues, as well. His wife had passed several years earlier from cancer, so he lived alone.

His only child, Lisa, helped out when she could, bringing him food, and walking Mickey. Lisa was in her late 30s, single with an active social life, and worked a regular job. With her busy schedule, she still made time for her father. Autumn didn't know Lisa that well, since they were ten years apart; she envied her in that she had the opportunity to take care of her dad. Autumn wished her parents could have lived long enough for her to help them out in their later years. They were only in their mid-50s when the accident took them from her.

"Where did this little bundle come from?" asked Steve.

"The shelter. It's hard to believe she came in this afternoon and I was the first one to see her. I got lucky."

"Definitely. Small breeds go fast. She was meant to be yours."

"Agreed."

"I've only ever had poodles, so I'm not familiar with Shih Tzus. Do you remember when I had the black and the white one? I loved walking them together."

"Yep. They looked so regal."

"With this even cut instead of the show cut, people don't recognize the breed. With so many poodle mixes, like golden doodle, cockapoo, people aren't used to seeing a purebred standard poodle. A woman asked me which breed Mickey is, and I told her that he's a 'Poodle doodle.' Steve chuckled.

Autumn thought that the standard-sized poodles were handsome, sweet, and well behaved, but hard to pick up and cuddle. Chrissy was the perfect size to be portable.

Mickey was a certified therapy dog. Steve brought him to visit nursing homes, libraries, and hospitals. Autumn wondered if Chrissy might make a good therapy dog one day. She was off to a good start in the way she handled Autumn's emotional flare-ups.

Ahead of them, Chrissy and Mickey trotted side-by-side, stopping from time to time to squat or to lift a leg.

"Her daddy passed away yesterday and his family didn't want her."

"So that would make it Sunday." Steve searched his memory. "There was something in the paper about an attorney who died. Gary Martin. My daughter works in his law office. She used to tell me all about how cute his dog was. He'd bring her to the office. He lived alone and his dog stayed with the body. I wonder if it's Chrissy."

"Brenda at the shelter said they found her next to the body. Did it say what he died of?"

"I'm not sure. The paper is in my recycling pile."

"I'd love to see it." Autumn's curiosity piqued, and she looked down at Chrissy, wanting to know more about her story.

"Lisa is coming over tomorrow after work. She can confirm whether Chrissy is, uh, was, Gary's dog."

"That'd be great."

ℂ

Back at the house, Autumn realized that her best friend, Stephanie Douglas, had no idea of Autumn's major life change of having a pet. She would clue her in before guilt got the better of her.

In the meantime, Autumn retrieved the two cushioned doggy beds from the bags, one pink and white and the other purple, and brought them into her bedroom. The room had been hers growing up, and had an adjoining bath. In her mind, the master bedroom was still her parents' room, so she maintained old habits and ways of moving about the house.

She clenched her fists to stop trembling, and refocused on the doggy beds. Her body eased a bit. She showed Chrissy her options. Chrissy briefly considered them, and jumped onto Autumn's queen-sized bed, picking the side opposite of where Autumn slept. She gazed at Autumn and put her head on the pillow.

"Okay. That works for me."

She smiled at Chrissy and put a little microfiber blanket over her. *So precious and sweet.* Autumn kissed Chrissy's head and got ready for bed, slipping in beside Chrissy without disturbing her. A faint odor of shelter disinfectant mixed with the fragrance of dog-romping-with-a-friend hit Autumn's nostrils. This pup was due for a shampoo, and she made a mental note to bathe Chrissy tomorrow. Snuggled with the dog in bed, Autumn picked up her Kindle and purchased a book about the personality, lore, care, and grooming of Shih Tzus, and started reading.

⇗ 3 ⇗

Ray Reed sat at his desk with a cup of black coffee and Ace curled up on the floor beside him. Getting into the office early gave him a head start on the day.

He pressed the power button and the phone flashed to life, a picture of Chrissy with pink bows in her hair sitting on a polished wood floor with the current time and date at the top. The account was still active. Ray scrolled through Gary's messages, including a message from his cell phone carrier reminding him of the monthly bill.

The last message Gary Martin ever sent was to someone named "Kitty." He scrolled down to see the conversation thread.

GM: Come over and we can talk about it.

Kitty: And if I do?

GM: We can work something out.

Kitty: OK

The date and time of the text indicated that he died the same evening. Gary Martin was expecting Kitty to come to his house. But when? Ray's mind ran through possible scenarios. If Kitty came after 7 pm, she would have discovered the body. Corinne Taylor's 911 call came in around noon the following day, leaving the possibilities that the mystery woman was Corinne Taylor, or that someone else found the body and did not report it, or Kitty never showed up in the first place. No matter which option was true, Gary Martin and Chrissy went undiscovered for an estimated 17 hours before someone came and notified the authorities.

He continued scrolling to see older texts but found none from Kitty. How had they met? How long had Gary Martin known Kitty? What was their relationship? Was it a romance, a friendship, or something else? Ray mentally processed the questions, each taking him in other directions.

He decided to look at Gary Martin's photos. Most of them were of Chrissy wearing different bows, and a couple of selfies with Gary and Chrissy. The others were of some women and their dogs or holding Chrissy. A few looked like they may be associated with legal cases he was working on, including one of a crushed four-door sedan and the scarred torso of a man.

Ray looked at his watch. The law office of Martin and Evans should be open by now.

∞

Autumn woke to the sun streaming through the divided light windows of her spacious bedroom. The light made the walls a lighter green than the evening version of the color, which was deep sage. As with every morning, her thoughts turned to her parents, habitually listening for a rustle of activity in the hallway that never came. Autumn sighed, trying to keep her grief at bay. She looked over to see Chrissy facing her, lying quietly. Autumn reached out and stroked her side, the sadness tempered by love for this furry blessing.

"Good morning, sweetheart."

Chrissy lazily blinked her eyes and gave a little wag. She stayed in bed while Autumn performed her morning routine. They moved into the kitchen and Autumn took a dose of anti-anxiety medication while Chrissy lapped up some water.

A knock on the door set Chrissy's tail wagging, and she let out a high-pitched bark. Autumn answered the door, her second cup of coffee in hand. Steve stood in the doorway, newspaper under his arm, with Mickey in tow.

"Morning!" Steve handed Autumn the paper. The aroma of coffee beckoned him.

"Hey, Steve. Hi, Mickey. Come on in."

The tails of both dogs wagged in high gear, as they sniffed each other in greeting.

"Mickey needs to go for his morning walk."

"How about we let them out back to play, and we can have coffee?"

Steve nodded his agreement. The two furry friends charged out through the sliding glass door and into the yard.

"Good thing my parents had the yard fenced. I didn't see the value at the time, but it's handy knowing Chrissy is safe outside."

"As small as she is, you want to keep an eye on her with the foxes, raccoons, and hawks in the area. Mickey will watch out for her when they're together. And she still needs regular walks. Let's have a cup and then take them around the neighborhood."

Autumn poured Steve a healthy serving into a handmade ceramic mug of deep blues and browns. He refused milk and sugar. Their wooden chairs scraped across the walnut-toned porcelain tile floor and they sat on the thick cushions Autumn's mother had sewed a couple of years ago. Every time Autumn sat on one, she saw her mother's smile welcoming her to sit down and chat. Tears threatened to come.

"It's hard losing your parents." Steve put a comforting hand on Autumn's arm.

Autumn had not realized her grief was outwardly apparent. She closed her eyes, took a deep breath, and felt her feet on the floor the way Dr. Wes instructed her to do. She knew Steve understood her pain.

"How long did it take you to get over losing your wife?"

"You never quite get over it. It's more about finding a way to remember all the good times without becoming emotional."

Autumn shook her head, pessimistic that she would get to that point any time soon.

"It's different for everyone," said Steve. "You'll be fine. You are just raw right now. Three months isn't that long. Give yourself a chance."

He patted Autumn's hand. She gave a weak nod, trying to believe him. His words and his presence brought some comfort.

Steve ruffled the newspaper and placed it on the table, opened to the story he had seen. It was a medium-sized article on page two with the headline, *Bucks County Attorney Found Dead.*

"This is the story I was telling you about."

Autumn took the paper and began to read.

"He was a criminal attorney and the family reported several items missing from the house, but they don't say what." Autumn continued to skim the article. "They mention a Shih Tzu found with him when they discovered the body. It must have been terrible for her."

"Yep. And it says cause of death to be determined, but there was never a follow-up story that I saw."

"Why was his death big news?"

"Gary Martin was the go-to guy for anyone who wanted the best criminal defense in the Philadelphia area. He was well-connected with politicians, local government, and, of course, criminals."

"I've never heard of him."

"Be glad that you haven't. It means you didn't need him." Steve smiled.

"May I keep this?"

Steve nodded.

"Let's retrieve Mickey and Chrissy and see if we can get them to take a walk."

They drained the last of the coffee from their mugs and opened the sliders to let the pups into the house.

ℬ

Ray walked into the law office of Martin and Evans accompanied by Ace. The legal assistants manning the desks in the reception area eyed them.

"May I help you?" said the woman closest to the door.

"Detective Reed to see Vaughn Evans."

"Do you have an appointment?" Her nameplate said *Lisa Coleman.*

"Lisa, we spoke on the phone yesterday about Mr. Martin's will."

"Yes, I remember. Let me see if Vaughn is available."

She picked up the phone receiver.

"*I'll* see if he's available," said a gruff voice from the other side of the room. She picked up her own receiver and angrily punched in the extension.

Ray looked at Lisa. She shrugged.

"Fran is Vaughn's secretary. I supported Gary."

Fran glared at Lisa while whispering to Vaughn.

"Vaughn will see you now. Follow me."

She rose up and strode down the hallway to a door with Vaughn's name etched on a brass nameplate. She knocked and opened the door for Ray.

He nodded at her and entered the office.

ॐ

The mile-and-a-half walk did both Chrissy and Autumn good. With every walk, Autumn got to know Chrissy better. Watching her gait, noting her habits, and seeing how she interacted with Mickey and the environment gave Autumn a barometer of Chrissy's mood. Her loss was only a couple of days ago, so Autumn wanted to be sensitive to her progress. Walks helped lessen the anxiety for both of them, plus it made Autumn's stomach flatter and her head clearer, nice side effects of this addition to her morning routine.

Chrissy waited inside the door for Autumn to remove her leash and harness and place them in the large basket earmarked for Chrissy's coats and walking accessories. They moved into the kitchen to get water, and then into the living room to go through Chrissy's possessions. Autumn retrieved the two bags of doggy treasures and dumped them out on the floor. Chrissy sat close by, interested in rediscovering her toys.

Stuffed squeaky toys in various shapes: a raccoon, a lion, a lamb, a rainbow-colored unknown creature, a monkey, and several well-used balls and chew bones were scattered on the floor. Chrissy shifted to a Sphinx position and observed, but did not make a move to play. Autumn looked at her and picked up the monkey, holding it closer to Chrissy. Chrissy put her head on her paws, so she put the monkey back on the pile. Since Chrissy chose Autumn's bed over her own, Autumn filled the purple doggy bed with toys and left the other one empty in case Chrissy wanted to use it.

22

The bag of clothing was next. Chrissy had coats for all kinds of weather and in all colors, some with faux fur collars, and some for wet weather. She also had a selection of T-shirts, sweaters, boots, and dresses. Autumn was amazed at the variety of styles of doggie clothing and accessories. She wanted to see which ones looked good on Chrissy and whether she liked wearing them.

Autumn systematically separated the items. She tried each piece of clothing on her and watched her reaction.

Chrissy did not like anything pulled over her head, so Autumn sorted those items and put them in a pile to give to the shelter. The coats had Velcro straps to make them easy to take on and off. Chrissy was more tolerant of these, but few looked good on her. The copper sheen coat with the leopard collar, for example. Chrissy didn't look happy wearing it, so Autumn tossed it into the giveaway pile. Many of the items were too big or too small, so she eliminated those as well. They ended up with several spring jackets in hot pink, black-and-white polka dots, and gray, one cute little dress with a rose on it, and a quilted snow jacket in deep pink. The shelter got the majority of the outfits, which was fine with Autumn and Chrissy.

Autumn gathered up the brushes and combs lined up next to the *keep* pile, along with a pair of hair scissors, and took Chrissy out on the patio.

"Can I brush you? You'll look so pretty."

Chrissy sat next to Autumn on the ground and allowed her to pull the wire brush through her long hair. The stress from recent events had been hard on Chrissy's coat, making it tangled and wiry. Autumn hit some snags and was careful not to pull too hard. She cut the thicker knots and then brushed through them. Autumn was determined to get her back to soft and gorgeous.

The mainly white coat accented by charcoal gray on Chrissy's back and head gave her a balanced look, the hair on both ears and eyes gray with the lower half of her face and beard white. The white tuft of hair on the top of her head was the star Autumn read about that was a Shih Tzu's signature put there by Buddha who bestowed a blessing with a kiss. Chrissy's patience and calm demeanor while Autumn brushed her made the interaction peaceful and served as a bonding activity for them both.

A pile of hair accumulated on the patio, filled with knots and loose hair from the brush, plus bits of grass from her outdoor excursions. Chrissy looked fluffier but still in need of a shampoo.

"How about a bath?"

Chrissy turned her head sideways and her ears perked up. The word was familiar but not one she liked. Her mouth turned down and her head lowered, resigned to her fate. Chrissy let Autumn pick her up and take her into the guest bathroom where the shower had a hand-held nozzle. She set the water to warm and noticed Chrissy wince at the sound of the water. She trembled slightly.

"It's okay."

Autumn tested the water temperature and began soaking Chrissy from head to tail while talking to her in a calm, gentle voice. She kept her head down and let the water run off her nose.

"What a good girl."

Chrissy shook too soon, spraying Autumn and the walls, and had to be drenched once again. Autumn warmed the organic honeysuckle shampoo between her palms and lathered up her fuzzy little girl. Chrissy let her, moving her paws and tail to Autumn's hands, shaking again, and spraying Autumn with suds. She laughed and petted Chrissy's head while she rinsed her off.

A thoroughly shampooed Shih Tzu emerged from the shower and once again blasted the white tiled walls and Autumn with excess water. Autumn grabbed the towels and threw them over Chrissy, trying to contain the burst. Chrissy shook off again and this time the towels absorbed most of the water. Autumn cooed assurances at Chrissy as she squeezed the water from her, the towels already soaked. Chrissy gave soft grunts as Autumn tended to her.

The blow dryer presented another challenge, with Chrissy trying to avoid the nozzle of warm air. She wondered how her former groomer had dealt with this issue or if the groomer had caused it from rough handling. With so much hair, it took almost thirty minutes to get Chrissy completely moisture free.

Autumn sat back after the final brushing and admired her work. Chrissy's hair was bright, white, and soft. Chrissy shook her flowing mane and looked pleased with herself. Autumn hugged her and kissed her head, the fragrance of organic honeysuckle shampoo a pleasant change from dirt and shelter disinfectant. It was not the same as the fresh honeysuckle carried on the late spring breeze, but it was close enough.

"Looks like I'll have to set aside at least 90 minutes to wash and dry you, little one."

Chrissy looked at Autumn with an expression that said, *I'm worth it.* Autumn's lack of experience with dogs made her uncertain as to whether it was common for them to have facial expressions, but she knew this one did. The endearing little face won her over every time she looked at her.

Autumn padded behind Chrissy, who sauntered into the kitchen to get a drink. Autumn heard her tongue lapping at the cool water as she picked up the paper Steve had brought earlier. Again, she read the headline: *Bucks County Attorney Found Dead.*

Criminal defense attorney Gary Martin, 40, from the law firm of Martin & Evans, LLC, was pronounced dead on arrival after being found on the floor of his Knollwood, Pennsylvania residence.

"You lived in the same town as me for the last three years?"

Chrissy's ears perked up and she tilted her head.

Corinne Taylor, a friend of the deceased, called 911 at noon after discovering Mr. Martin face down in his entry foyer. Ms. Taylor claims that his Shih Tzu sat next to the body refusing to move, and she promptly called the police. Detective Raymond Reed of the Knollwood Police Department said the medical examiner estimates Mr. Martin's time of death at 17 hours earlier; cause unknown at this time. Clients of Mr. Martin's law practice will continue to be served by his partner, Vaughn Evans. A private funeral is scheduled. Please donate to the Society for the Prevention of Cruelty to Animals in lieu of flowers.

"My devoted little girl." Autumn reached down and rubbed Chrissy's head. It was nice to have her near.

Autumn put the newspaper down and called Chrissy to follow her to the purple dog bed filled with toys, and brought it into the living room. She patted her leg to get Chrissy's interest. She came over and sat next to Autumn but did not engage with her toys or the idea of play. Autumn caressed her little body, moving her hand gently over her back.

She picked up the squeaky lion and held it up to Chrissy, squeezing the toy so it made noise. Chrissy put her head on her paws. Autumn tried the raccoon with the same result. She fished around in the doggy bed looking for a ball under the pile of stuffed dog toys and threw it, but Chrissy stayed put. Autumn retrieved the ball.

She mindlessly tossed the ball up and caught it, watching Chrissy, and wondering if she could get more information about Gary Martin and anything that had to do with Chrissy. Autumn was curious about Gary's cause of death and Chrissy's experience in those final moments, knowing that would help her care for Chrissy in the best possible way.

It was almost four o'clock. Autumn's best friend, Stephanie Douglas, was likely home from Knollwood Elementary School, where she taught fifth grade. It was time to introduce Stephanie and Chrissy. She also wanted to talk it over with Stephanie before heading to the police station tomorrow and asking for Detective Reed. She picked up her own phone and dialed Stephanie's number.

"Hey, Autumn!"

Stephanie's upbeat, welcoming greeting was always good for a pick-me-up.

"How was your day?"

"The kids were amazing. They grasp information so fast."

Autumn admired Stephanie's dedication to the kids and their wellbeing.

"I'm sure it's because they have a great teacher. Are you available for dinner?"

"Would love to. Your place or mine or out?"

"Let's do takeout and come have it at my place. There's someone I want you to meet."

"You're not trying to fix me up again, are you?"

Autumn laughed, remembering the last time she'd tried to play matchmaker. It was a disaster. Stephanie made her promise never to do it again. She conceded.

"Nothing like that, I swear."

"Does 5:30 sound good?"

"Perfect. See you then."

She hung up, thinking that if they had wanted to go to a restaurant she could not have brought Chrissy. She had not filed the paperwork. Her father's voice rang in her head saying, *there's no time like the present.* Autumn pulled up the registration website for emotional support animals. Armed with her letter from Dr. Wes, she filled out the online form, bought Chrissy her official ESA gear in pink, and received a temporary registration card to download until her official papers came in the mail. This, plus medical certification, should suffice if questioned about bringing a dog into places that normally do not allow them.

"You're all set, sweetheart."

Chrissy looked at Autumn and smiled at her. Was she seeing things? Wishful thinking? Chrissy was smart and engaging, but these facial expressions were incredible. She would see if Stephanie noticed it, too. Autumn would also ask Dr. Wes if her anti-anxiety medication could cause this type of hallucination. Speaking of which, it was time to take her evening dose.

৪০

"To what do I owe the pleasure, Detective?" Vaughn said without looking up from his work.

Vaughn's impressive diploma from the University of Pennsylvania Law School hung prominently on the wall behind his desk. His demeanor carried the weight of his Ivy League education. Law books filled six-foot long bookcases against both walls, the cliché décor of an attorney's office. His engraved brass nameplate matched the outside signage.

"I'm here regarding the death of your partner."

"I thought it was a heart attack."

"Where did you get that idea?"

"From Gary's sister."

Ray made a note that Vaughn Evans and Anna Martin had spoken.

"What was the conversation about?"

"The will and next steps."

"What was her demeanor when you spoke with her?"

"I'm sorry, Detective, that falls under attorney-client privilege."

Ray nodded.

"How are you feeling about Gary's death?"

"Disappointed. He was a good attorney who should have taken better care of himself."

"Was there anything you noticed about Mr. Martin on the day of his death?"

"I didn't see him that day. It was Sunday. I don't normally interact with him on weekends."

Ray noticed that Vaughn did not fall for his trick question.

"What did you do on Sunday?"

"Spent a quiet day at home...with no one to corroborate my whereabouts, if that's what you're wondering." Vaughn smirked.

"Have you noticed anything unusual about Gary in the past week prior to his death?"

"He was under stress as usual. The incident with Travis Mitchell didn't help, of course."

"Travis Mitchell?" Ray wrote down the name.

"We filed a police report. The guy practically attacked Gary for missing a filing deadline. Right here in the office."

"What type of service was Mr. Martin providing to Mr. Mitchell?"

"Criminal defense for a drug dealing charge. It's been filed with the court, so you can check it out yourself."

"What was the nature of your relationship with Mr. Martin?"

"He was my business partner."

"Did you get along?"

"As well as any business partners do."

Ray picked up on the blocking techniques and decided to end the interview for now.

"Thank you for your time, Mr. Evans."

Vaughn Evans had already gone back to his work and grunted a goodbye as Ray rose and headed out the door.

༄

Stephanie was on time as usual. Her signature knock of three quick raps followed by two farther apart made Chrissy growl and bark at the door, ruining the surprise. Chrissy's voice was different from when she welcomed Mickey and Steve. This was more of a warning. Autumn vowed to pay closer attention to Chrissy's inflections to understand her signals. She unlocked the bolt and saw Stephanie's light pink mouth agape and one hand with matching pale pink nails holding her chest over strands of light brown hair. She tentatively entered the foyer, white sneakers squeaking on the tile floor.

"It's okay, Chrissy. This is your aunt, Stephanie."

Chrissy sat down and looked at her. Stephanie handed Autumn a large container of her special, low-sugar lemonade and knelt down to Chrissy's level. Autumn took the bottle and put it in the fridge while they got acquainted. Stephanie held out her hand, letting Chrissy get used to her scent. Chrissy sniffed Stephanie's hand. Familiarity established, Stephanie stroked Chrissy's soft head.

"She's beautiful!"

Autumn smiled; glad she'd taken the time to groom her before Stephanie met her. She walked back out thrilled to see Stephanie running her fingers over Chrissy's soft belly.

"When did you decide to get a dog?"

"Yesterday. It was Dr. Wes' idea. I wasn't sure I would do it. Then I met this one and the decision was easy."

At the sight of Autumn, Chrissy stood up and wagged her tail. She held out her hands, and Chrissy allowed her to lift and snuggle her.

"I'll say. You two look like you belong together."

Autumn smiled and gave Chrissy a kiss before putting her down. They walked into the kitchen, where the usual menus from local restaurants that delivered spread across the kitchen counter.

"Here. Check out our options."

Stephanie glanced at Chrissy's feeding area. "Crystal bowls? Seriously?"

Autumn smiled. "They were with her other things. Besides, they're perfect for this little princess."

Stephanie shook her head and chose Thai. They placed their order, poured some lemonade, and went out onto the patio. They watched as Chrissy ran in the grass and sniffed the bushes. She had grown fond of hunting chipmunks but probably would not have any idea what to do with it if she caught one.

"She seems comfortable here."

"I'm doing my best. But she has a long way to go. She's grieving."

"How do you know that?"

"She barely eats and doesn't want to play with her toys."

"Maybe it's just getting used to the new place," Stephanie suggested.

"It feels different from that. The woman at the shelter told me her daddy died a couple days ago. My neighbor, Steve, also brought me the paper with the story in it."

"It was in the paper? So this dog is famous?"

Autumn nodded.

"More or less. Her pet parent's death was the main story. That's only half of it. She also has separation anxiety."

"Incredible. Only you could find a dog with the same problems you're having. No wonder you two understand each other."

Autumn nodded and took a sip of her lemonade. Stephanie made the best. The evening sun beamed through the leaves of the silver maple that towered over the rooftop.

"Let me get the article."

She went into the house just as the doorbell rang. She paid for the food and put the bags on the counter. Newspaper in hand, she went back outside and handed it to Stephanie.

"Check this out while I get plates and stuff."

Stephanie took the paper and began reading while Autumn retrieved utensils, plates, napkins, and the food, making a couple of trips to ensure none of it ended up on the ground. Her periodic clumsiness ensured that she could never support herself as a waiter. She placed Chrissy's bowls on a placemat near her chair. Stephanie looked up from the paper.

"Wow. So they don't know what killed him."

"Not as far as I know, but I intend to find out."

"What do you mean?"

"Something doesn't feel right about the death."

"It could have been a heart attack."

"The guy was too young for something like that."

Stephanie scrunched her mouth in thought.

"High stress job, single – men don't do well on their own the way women can. Without knowing about his personal habits and diet, it's a toss-up as to whether or not he was a candidate for cardiac arrest."

"Point taken, but I have a gut feeling about it," said Autumn.

"Like the feeling you had about the guy you tried to fix me up with?"

Stephanie gave Autumn a look punctuated with two raised eyebrows and a smirk.

"Will you ever let me live that down? So I got that one wrong."

"That's an understatement!"

Autumn smiled at the memory of Stephanie's report of the infamous date. The guy took her to an Italian restaurant, talked her ear off about his entire personal history, and then tried to dine and dash to avoid paying the check. His name was Don, and the name became a secret code between the two women synonymous with dud.

"This is different."

"How is this different?"

"It seems like Chrissy is trying to tell me that her daddy's death wasn't from natural causes."

Stephanie took a bite of shrimp pad Thai and wiped her hands on the napkin before taking it.

"Are you kidding me? The dog is telling you?"

"I can't explain it. She has a way about her that lets me know what she's thinking."

Autumn shoveled rice and vegetables soaked in panang curry into her mouth. Stephanie looked at her, one eyebrow raised. Autumn hated when she did that. One eyebrow was the signal to drop something before it became a problem. Two raised brows symbolized admonishment.

"I'm going to the police station tomorrow."

"And tell them what?"

"That I'm Chrissy's new pet parent and I want to know what she went through when Gary Martin died."

"I doubt they'll care."

"It's important for me to find out more. For Chrissy's sake."

Chrissy looked up at Autumn and smiled.

"Did she just smile?"

Autumn was relieved that Stephanie saw it too, and nodded.

"Astounding. Let me know if the police think you're bonkers."

"I will, thanks for your support, Steph."

Stephanie pushed her empty plate away. "Do we have anything for dessert?"

⸝ 4 ⸜

Autumn and Chrissy entered the Knollwood Police Station and went up to the counter. A receptionist sat behind glass with a voice port to enable communication. They were the only ones in the waiting area. Not much happened in Knollwood until recently, despite its proximity to Philadelphia. Gary Martin's death was the biggest news in the last twenty years, besides the crash that killed her parents.

"Hello. I'd like to speak with Detective Reed, please."

"And you are?" said the receptionist.

"Autumn Clarke."

"What is this regarding?"

"The death of Gary Martin."

The receptionist looked a bit shocked and tried to cover her surprise.

"Have a seat."

Ten minutes passed before a fit, dark-haired detective with a boyish face greeted them.

"Autumn Clarke?"

"Yes."

"Ray Reed."

A broad smile welcomed her, and he extended his hand.

Autumn had butterflies in her stomach and put her hand over it to keep them at bay. His authoritative stance, shoulder holster, and solid build pressing against his white dress shirt and blue striped tie made her stare a moment longer than she intended.

"Nice tie."

"Thanks. A gift from my mother. Please come with me."

She liked that he had a relationship with his mom.

He led them back to his desk. Autumn was surprised no one objected to Chrissy's presence. They sat in a chair across from Detective Reed's desk, Chrissy calm and comfortable in Autumn's lap.

"She looks familiar."

"This is Chrissy. I adopted her a couple of days ago and discovered she belonged to Gary Martin."

"I was at the scene. I remember her. She cried and barked when we took her away from the body. I was surprised no one in the family was interested in keeping her."

"Me, too! Their loss is my gain."

31

Reed nodded and petted Chrissy's head.

"I'm glad she found a good home so quickly. Is she the reason you're here about Gary Martin's death?"

"Yes. I'd like information about Chrissy and her experience. She seems depressed."

A police officer came into the bullpen with a dignified black and tan German shepherd dog, and Chrissy perked up.

"Can she say hello?" asked Autumn.

Reed gave the okay.

Autumn put her on the floor and let out the retractable leash. Chrissy approached the much bigger dog. Their tails wagged, and they sniffed each other fervently without incident. Autumn wished she were as good at making friends as Chrissy was.

"Thanks for walking him for me," said Reed as the officer handed him the leash.

The police officer nodded and left the room, leaving the German shepherd dog behind.

"His name is Ace."

Reed tied the leather leash to his desk drawer handle.

"He's beautiful," said Autumn.

"Thanks. We served in the K-9 unit together. He's been with me ever since, about six years. Ace is retired as an officer, but the department recognized our bond and let me keep him."

"That's great. Sounds like he's a partner you can trust."

"With my life."

Chrissy and Ace sat on the floor near each other but not touching, comfortable in a way Autumn wanted to feel in her own relationships. Autumn watched them. When she turned back, she caught Reed watching her.

"I can't release details of the investigation."

"There's an investigation? Has the cause of death been determined?"

"What makes you think it wasn't?"

"Your quote from the newspaper."

"You can't believe everything you read." Ray gave her a gleaming, sly smile.

His dismissiveness was irritating. Reed pushed a contact card for Autumn to fill out across his desk.

"In case we need to get a hold of you."

She complied, somewhat annoyed by Reed's change of demeanor. A man open when talking about his dog, but closed about his work. She hoped he would contact her about the case and whatever else he wanted to talk about.

"Thank you for coming in and making us aware of Chrissy's good fortune, Ms. Clarke."

"Autumn, please."

"Autumn." He leaned in a bit, almost touching her hand as he took the contact card, and gave her a relaxed smile.

"That's it?"

"That's it. For now."

Reed stood up, signaling the end of the meeting. Autumn petted Ace and tugged Chrissy to her feet, disappointed in the anti-climactic meeting.

Autumn decided to try one last tactic. Turning to Reed, she smiled.

"I'm new to having a dog and am thinking of taking her to a dog park. Are there any you recommend?"

"The best one is over on Sycamore Street across from the elementary school."

She waited a beat, hoping he would invite Chrissy for a playdate with Ace. With nothing forthcoming, she said thanks, held her hand up in a brief wave, and turned to leave.

૪૭

Detective Reed watched them leave, noting Chrissy's tiny steps and paying special attention to Autumn's figure and long, shiny auburn hair. Her bright blue eyes enthralled him. He wondered if he should have asked them to the dog park.

Ray had never been a fast mover when it came to relationships, but there was something intriguing about Autumn Clarke. Moreover, Ace seemed to like Chrissy.

He was in unfamiliar territory. His heart leapt when he saw this slender, attractive woman with a little dog in tow. He liked the way she filled out her jeans and pink T-shirt. Her precise penmanship and smooth hand with neat, natural manicure gave the impression of a careful, articulate individual. Reed's training made it hard to turn off the profiling part of his brain.

Saying her first name elevated his mood, and though he tried not to show it, he worried that she noticed his interest.

He turned his attention to Gary Martin's file. It was murder, but he could not share that with Autumn. Not yet.

Ray opened his computer and searched Autumn's name in the database. The brutal accident from three months prior popped onto the screen. The truck driver and Autumn's parents all dead at the scene. It was a miracle that she had survived.

෨

Autumn loaded Chrissy into her safety seat and then got behind the wheel, gripped it, and banged her head on her hands. Did she think the police would give her information about the case? That her fluttering insides were somehow a sign that Detective Reed showed interest in her? How stupid. She looked at Chrissy, who was staring at her, seeming to wonder why Autumn was making a banging sound with her head. Autumn reached back and petted Chrissy.

"Sorry you've been through so much. We need to find out what happened to your daddy."

Chrissy wagged her tail and snorted. Autumn put the car in drive and headed home.

That night, Autumn tossed and turned, thoughts of Gary lying on the floor, Chrissy's distress, and Ray Reed. His face floated across her mind once or twice, making her wonder if there was a chance of seeing him again. It had been almost a year since her relationship with Scott Anderson had ended, leaving her with a sour taste in her mouth and reluctance toward getting involved with another man. Somehow, Ray seemed different. She pushed the thoughts aside.

Chrissy whimpered in her sleep and shuddered in the wake of a bad dream. The trauma of witnessing her daddy's death was bad enough. Having no choice but to stay with the body for an entire night and half of the next day made it worse. They were both dealing with parental death, but at least Autumn knew the cause of her parents' demise.

As Autumn rocked and snuggled Chrissy, she was more committed than ever to taking care of her new fur baby and to finding out how her daddy died, police help or not.

⩵5⩵

With the morning routine that now included Chrissy's needs accomplished, Autumn went into her second-floor office. She had taken over the far spare bedroom off the wide upstairs hallway. Visits to her office had been scarce over the last three months, because it had to pass her mother's sewing room.

Her mother had taken the middle spare bedroom for this use. The sound of her mother's Singer sewing machine beating a tune as she made pillow covers, curtains, and other décor for the house used to disrupt her thoughts as she worked. Now the silence disquieted her more than the noise.

Despite the reluctance of going by the empty room, Chrissy's situation gave her purpose. Sunlight splashed against pale yellow walls. Cream-white bookcases lined two of them and her whitewashed oak desk with a beige upholstered office chair welcomed her back.

Chrissy sat next to her in an old swivel executive chair pumped high enough for her to see out of the open window. She was the picture of comfort, poised in her pink and white doggie bed, a perfect fit on the chair's seat. Chrissy rested her head on the padded arm and quietly observed her new yard; a light breeze blew across her bangs. Her little snorting noises and periodic snoring filled the too-quiet house and made Autumn smile.

The Google search for Gary Martin proved fruitful as news stories populated the screen. Most of them were about the death, reiterating the same information she had learned from the newspaper article. Some stories covered court cases. Martin had defended some seedy characters. She was looking for something else, a tidbit of information that provided a new lead, or even Gary Martin's address.

She scrolled down, looking at the brief summaries of each story and found an entry about Martin's death with a "formerly residing at" address. And there it was – 425 Carversville Drive. It was in a neighborhood about five minutes from where Autumn lived. The houses there were gated executive homes built about ten years ago, considered new for the area. Since then, building had come to a halt to preserve the forested village of Knollwood. Mr. Martin must have made a good living to enable him to purchase a home there.

She wrote down the address and plugged it into a real estate search site. Photos of the inside and outside of the house filled the screen. She wondered about the speed of the listing posted online. Gary Martin's family must really want the house sold in a hurry.

Autumn enlarged the photos and clicked through them, assessing each one. Marble and hardwood graced various rooms while luxurious carpets and rugs donned others. The high-end kitchen and sophisticated décor throughout the house looked like a spread in a design magazine.

She pictured the foyer with the body on the floor, noting how close it might have been to the entryway table. The virtual tour of the property gave her some idea of the floorplan.

"What a beautiful house you lived in!"

Chrissy gazed at Autumn out from under her long bangs, her deep brown eyes tinged with sadness.

When she turned back to the computer screen, the listing realtor's face loomed to the right. Autumn preferred dealing with familiar folks in this case. Her mother had a realtor friend, but she did not remember her name. Stella Clarke used to accompany the realtor to check out her new listings. She loved to look at houses even though she would not dream of selling their family home.

Autumn stood and Chrissy went on alert, expecting to go wherever she was heading. Autumn lifted Chrissy from her perch and placed her on the floor. Chrissy shook and followed her down the upstairs hall. At the door to the master suite, Autumn paused. She always kept their door closed to maintain what Autumn considered her parents' energy signature. She wanted the scent of their cologne and bath products preserved as long as possible. She opened the door a crack. Chrissy sat upright at Autumn's feet waiting for instructions.

"You can't come in, sweetheart."

Chrissy's mouth turned down, but she obeyed. From the doorway, Autumn saw Mom's address book on her nightstand, where she always kept it. She hesitated before crossing the threshold, savoring the dissipating scent of her parents. She grabbed the book and closed the door gently behind her.

She clutched the book to her chest, tears coming, wishing that her mother were there to tell her the name of the realtor. Chrissy pushed her head against Autumn's leg and looked up. Autumn met her deep, dark eyes and saw the concern there.

"I'm okay. Let's go sit on the couch."

Chrissy followed Autumn downstairs into the living room where they both made themselves comfortable. Autumn sat in the corner of the gushy couch and Chrissy draped herself over the back of it to peer at the front yard out of the large, divided light window that took up half of the outer wall. Autumn started at the beginning and flipped through her mother's address book until she found a card for Maureen Roberts, the realtor. She dialed the cell number, and Maureen answered on the second ring.

"Knollwood Realty. This is Maureen."

"Hi Maureen. This is Autumn Clarke."

"So good to hear from you, Autumn. How are you getting along?"

"As well as can be expected."

"I miss your mother. She was such good company."

"You and me both. I was wondering if you'd show me a house."

"Of course. Which property are you interested in?"

"425 Carversville Drive."

"Gary Martin's place? I don't mean to pry, but what would you want with that house? A body was found there! Your mother would never forgive me."

"It's a long story. Can we schedule a showing? I'm flexible."

"Of course, dear. How about tomorrow at 2 pm?"

"Perfect. I'll meet you there."

Autumn hung up, excited about the idea of going inside the house. She forgot to mention that Chrissy would be tagging along, but Maureen would probably allow it as a favor. Besides, it used to be Chrissy's house. It would be interesting to see how she reacted. She entered the appointment onto her calendar.

"Time for a walk, little one."

She put Chrissy's harness and leash on her and walked in the opposite direction of Steve and Mickey's house. Chrissy started whimpering when another dog appeared half a block up. It was their neighbor, Julie Hall, and Teddy, her Yorkshire terrier who was two-thirds Chrissy's size. The two canines rushed toward each other, pulling their mommies behind them despite their diminutive statures. They wasted no time sniffing one another.

"When did you get a dog?" Julie was a little out of breath from the sprint but her short, reddish brown hair stayed in perfect order.

"A couple of days ago. Doctor's orders. This is Chrissy. She's been great and very helpful keeping me sane."

Julie knew about Autumn's challenges and treatment plan, so she was comfortable sharing Chrissy's role in her recovery. She valued Julie's work history as a former nurse administrator in the adult psychiatric unit at the hospital. Julie's understanding of Autumn's condition was non-judgmental. Even her own research of her condition showed that her symptoms overlapped between PTSD – post-traumatic stress disorder – a clinically diagnosed mental illness that can last for years, versus PTS, which is a normal reaction to trauma and has temporary symptoms.

Julie petted Chrissy with enthusiasm. Chrissy looked away from Teddy long enough to acknowledge the compliment and then focused her attention back on the Yorkie.

"Looks like she's made another friend."

"Who is the other one?"

"Mickey. Let's all walk together sometime."

She pictured Ace and Ray joining them, and a grin spread across her face.

"Yes. Teddy and Mickey get along great."

Autumn admired Julie. Holding a doctorate in nursing got her promoted into the executive ranks at Bucks County General Hospital. The position brought regular hours into Julie's busy schedule and allowed her to take care of her two teenaged girls and her husband, Brad, a ranger at nearby Tyler State Park and the Peabody Conservancy, a public area donated by Horatio Peabody in the early 1900s.

The four of them strolled down the street, Chrissy and Teddy trying to outdo each other with marking their territory. The fragrance of honeysuckle filled the air as they walked past the vines growing on the split-rail fence. It seemed to spread everywhere this time of year, bringing with it wonderful memories of spring the sweet aroma triggered.

"Have you heard about the attorney found dead in his house?"

"Yes, I saw it on the news."

"Well he was Chrissy's daddy."

"What! How did you get her?"

"I adopted her at the shelter. They told me Martin's family didn't want her so she ended up in a cage."

"How horrible!"

"Unless you believe everything happens for a reason. I think she was supposed to be with me. She's got an uncanny sense of what to do when I have an episode and pulls me right out of it."

"Extraordinary. And I'm sure she's thrilled to be out of the shelter."

"Yes, I got her the same day she arrived."

"Good timing."

"She has separation anxiety. Not everyone wants to deal with that. For me, it's perfect. I signed her up to be an emotional support animal so I can keep her with me wherever I go."

"Certainly sounds like a match made in heaven."

Julie had no idea how divinely ordained it was.

"I'm confident that you're doing everything in your power to overcome these challenges. And what a great little companion. She's adorable."

"Thanks, Julie."

Autumn wanted to steer the conversation back to Gary Martin.

"Any information you can share about Gary Martin's death?"

"Well, Pennsylvania has a Right-to-Know Law granting public access to the deceased's name and the cause and manner of death. The Coroner's Act makes autopsy reports public records, as are death certificates. The results may take some time to upload into the system. His autopsy took place at Bucks General. I'm friends with the medical examiner, and he told me that the cause of death was an overdose of a lethal street drug called fentanyl."

Julie's circle of friends included everyone who met her. She was open and gregarious. Autumn allowed her to continue.

"I'm also friendly with one of the secretaries at his law firm, Fran Barnes. We had lunch the day after it happened, and she's pretty broken up about it."

"What did she say?"

"That he was stressed out, but she never expected him to keel over from a heart attack."

"So she was told it was natural causes?"

"I'm not sure what made her draw that conclusion. Nothing on the news said otherwise. I didn't want to tell her it was drug-related."

"With a drug involved, it begs the question of how he got it and when he took it. Most people don't walk through their front door and take drugs in the foyer. I have a hunch there's more to it. I'm going to find out what."

"How exciting! It'll be like the time you tracked down the thief who stole the proceeds from the silent auction at your mother's fundraiser. Who suspected that Mrs. Perkins was so hot to cruise to Greece but couldn't afford it? People still talk about how you saved the day."

"That was simpler than solving a murder. I was familiar with the suspects. I'm flying blind with this case."

"Let me know if I can help."

"How about lunch with you and your secretary friend? My place?"

"Sounds lovely."

A low rumble of thunder gave warning as the heavy clouds rolled in, darkening the sky. The leash vibrated in her hand, and Chrissy sat on the sidewalk shaking. Autumn scooped her up and waved goodbye to Julie and Teddy as they made a beeline for the house, making it inside as the first raindrops fell.

Another rumble of thunder and Chrissy was beside herself, panting and quivering. Autumn unhooked her leash and removed her harness, then gathered her up in her arms and headed for the couch where she surrounded them both with blankets and fluffy pillows. She held Chrissy to her chest and rocked her.

The panting became more tortured, saliva dripped onto Autumn's arm as rain pounded the roof and wind shook the trees. A nearby napkin came in handy to dry Autumn's arm and to soak up the moisture on Chrissy's beard and chest. She related to Chrissy's terror and attempted to distract her the way Chrissy had taken Autumn's attention from her own panic attacks. No squeaky toy, brushing, hugging, or coaxing worked. The poor baby was lost in the anxiety zone. It was hours before the storm finally subsided and the two of them drifted off to an exhausted sleep.

꞊6꞊

Autumn lifted Chrissy out of her car seat and placed her on the ground. Dr. Wes' office was about twenty minutes from the house, a longer ride than usual for Chrissy, and so a good stretch was in order. Chrissy shook and then extended first her front paws and then each rear leg in turn. It reminded Autumn of the yoga posture, "downward dog." Chrissy executed the moves like a master, and it made Autumn laugh.

Autumn guided her through the glass doors and into her psychiatrist's office. The receptionist gave a warm welcome and petted Chrissy. They took a seat in the waiting area. Chrissy, cooperative and quiet, sat at Autumn's feet. Autumn reached for a fashion magazine, thinking a new look would help capture Detective Reed's attention. Dr. Wes appeared in the doorway before she could peruse the latest fashions.

"Well, who do we have here?"

Chrissy wagged her tail and let Dr. Wes pet her head.

"This is Chrissy."

"How long have you had her?"

"This is day five. She's a rescue."

Autumn took a seat with Chrissy following her to the chair and stretching out on the floor at Autumn's feet. Dr. Wes nodded his approval.

"Looks like you're getting along just fine."

"Better than fine. She understands me. We have the same problems."

"Tell me more about that."

"She has separation anxiety. She shakes and drools when it thunders."

"It's called Astraphobia. Does it also occur during heavy rain?"

"It's possible given the downpour during the last storm."

Dr. Wes nodded his head.

"Many dogs experience this fear. Ask your veterinarian to recommend something that might help her. Do you know anything about her history?"

"Her pet parent was found dead last weekend. She had been by his side overnight until someone found them."

"It certainly sounds like what you're going through. Loss of a parent, post-traumatic stress, panic attacks."

Autumn told Dr. Wes in detail about her recent panic episodes.

"She's already pulled me out of a couple panic situations and brought me back to center."

"Smart little girl, aren't you, Chrissy?"

Chrissy beat her tail against the floor, her bright eyes connecting with Dr. Wes. Autumn saw Dr. Wes pull back as Chrissy met his gaze.

"Intense, isn't she?"

"I'll say. The way she made eye contact startled me.

Autumn smiled as she pet Chrissy with calm, loving strokes.

"Tell me about your relationship with Chrissy."

"I'm surprised at how quickly I've become attached. I thought those days were gone."

"What is your reaction to this sense of attachment?"

"It's like my heart reopened. I love waking up and having her there."

"So her presence elevates your mood?"

"More than that. She gives me hope that things will get better."

"Excellent! She seems connected to you, given your description of how she's aware of your attacks."

"Her awareness is uncanny. Dr. Wes, is it possible for my meds to cause hallucinations?"

"It's possible. Can you describe what you're experiencing?"

"I keep thinking Chrissy is making human expressions and communicating with me."

"Dogs are expressive and keen observers. They have their own way of imparting what they want and how they're feeling. Maybe you're tuning into Chrissy's way of conveying what she needs."

"It's beyond that. Chrissy's ability to let me know what she's thinking is peculiar."

"Give me an example."

"I can feel when she's sad or when she's worried about me. I know why she doesn't want to eat or play. And I sense the reasons she likes something or doesn't. It's as though we're tuned to the same frequency. But the biggest thing is her face. The way she smiles or looks upset. I must be imagining it."

Dr. Wes nodded. "I understood, having had a momentary taste of Chrissy's ability to connect in a way I've never experienced with other dogs."

He answered her original question. "While the drug could be modifying your perception on some level, it seems more likely you have developed an empathic connection with Chrissy."

"What does that mean?"

"Your sense of each other is strong, even though you have only been together less than a week. You both understand anxiety and how one another expresses it, tuning into each other's distress. Dogs especially have the ability to observe and respond appropriately to their pet parent's needs."

Autumn considered this explanation. It could account for part of it, but not the way Chrissy helped her understand *why* she trembled or was excited. Dr. Wes could see Autumn was skeptical of his interpretation of the situation.

He added, "At the same time, it could be coupled with a telepathic sense. There have been documented cases of animal communication going beyond simple behavioral cues."

Autumn nodded. She was not crazy, after all.

"She talks to me with various sounds she makes, and I've been able to decipher the meaning to an extent, like a high-pitched bark for her friends or a deeper bark for a stranger. But when she becomes intense, it's like she sends me a signal."

"Keep track of this type of interaction between you. We can go deeper on this topic next time. What else has been going on?"

"I'm worried that it's been three months later and, despite therapy and medication, my symptoms persist. I still have the guilt of surviving the crash. The grief over losing my parents overwhelms me on a daily basis, making it hard to get through the day."

"On a scale of one to ten, how much distress did you feel initially?"

"Ten."

"And now?"

"Since Chrissy, a seven."

"One degree for each month. That's progress. If you had said you're still at a ten, then we'd be having a different conversation."

"I guess."

"You feel as though you should be over it by now?"

Autumn looked down, feeling silly.

"I guess not. Three months isn't that long."

"No, it's not. Besides, in one week you've unexpectedly opened to having love in your life. Chrissy is a miracle worker."

"True. Nothing else makes me feel as good as she does. And it makes me happy to help her through her crisis, too."

"That's the key. The joy that comes from being loving and giving is something that no medication or therapy can bring. Give yourself credit for how far you've come in less than a week. You're definitely on the right track."

"It feels that way," Autumn said. Her mood lifted at the validation of her progress.

Dr. Wes looked at his watch. "Our time is up for this week. Continue paying attention to Chrissy and monitoring your thoughts. Stop them when they become painful and replace them with loving thoughts toward yourself, Chrissy, and the memory of your parents. He turned to Chrissy. "It was a pleasure meeting you, Chrissy."

Chrissy met his eyes, wagged her tail, and grunted. Autumn looked at the surprise in Dr. Wes' face and smiled.

≈7≈

The therapy sessions always ended on time, but the traffic was not as predictable. Knollwood was a cut-through to the popular New Hope area and tourists used the main road on a regular basis.

"We're going to your old house. But don't worry; your home is with me now and forever."

Autumn looked at Chrissy in the rearview mirror. The fuzzy little head lifted and she stared back into the mirror.

She adhered to the local twenty-five miles per hour speed limit. It gave Autumn a chance to get a sense of the neighborhood. One house after the other was big and beautiful with formal landscaping and circular driveways. She figured most of the folks who lived around here must be at work to support these executive mansions.

She passed a couple of people walking on the sidewalk, one with and one without a dog. Chrissy yelped when she saw the corgi in a tone reserved for recognition rather than warning.

"Is she a friend of yours?"

Chrissy made a murmuring noise in response.

Gary Martin's house came up on the right. Chrissy let out a whimper and started to shake.

"You okay?"

Autumn pulled to the side and put the car in park. She reached back to rub her.

A "For Sale" sign was on the strip of lawn near the street. She waited before pulling in, with Chrissy reliving her nightmare. She knew all too well what a panic attack was like. Her gaze shifted from the former Martin residence and turned back to the road. A car came charging around the corner, whizzing past her. Autumn's shock triggered an episode of shaking and hyperventilating, her chest heaving, and tears welling up. She gripped the wheel to quell the upsurge of panic.

Chrissy let out a series of sharp barks. Through her alarm and somewhere at the edge of panic, Autumn was able to focus on Chrissy's voice. Her rapid, shallow breath deepened and her grip on the wheel loosened. She reached back to connect with Chrissy's warm, soft body. It had a grounding effect, and Autumn's attack ended in a sigh and a deep breath. She felt her feet on the floor to even out her energy. *Thanks for the tip, Dr. Wes. Thanks, Chrissy.*

"We can't both be upset at the same time. We have to take turns," she said.

A few deep breaths later, Autumn put the car in gear and headed up the driveway, checking on Chrissy in the rearview mirror. Her little body trembled now that Autumn's crisis was over.

Maureen waved from the doorway. She greeted Autumn with a warm hug. The vivacious realtor was the most successful in the area. Her designer suit, expensive jewelry, blonde hair coiffed to perfection, and late model BMW yelled success to anyone who met her. Maureen's small stature belied her big personality.

"Let me look at you," Maureen exclaimed and held Autumn at arm's length. "You look so much like your mother."

"Thank you," Autumn smiled and moved her mind away from thinking too long about Stella Clarke.

Chrissy barked from the back seat of the Mercedes.

"Okay, I'm coming."

She lifted Chrissy from her car seat and noticed the trembling had subsided now that there was a new person to check out. She cradled Chrissy in her arms while Maureen reached out and petted her.

"Who's this? I'm not sure a dog can come into the house."

"This one can. It used to be her house."

"This is the dog who found Gary Martin dead?"

"No, she stayed with him until he was found by a friend."

"Oh. Well come in. Both of you."

Autumn let Chrissy walk into her former residence, wearing her leash. In the imposing two-story foyer with large, shiny marble tiles where they'd found Gary Martin, Chrissy began to whimper. Autumn picked her up and snuggled her close. Chrissy's small furry body trembled, and she whispered in Chrissy's ear to calm her.

If Autumn had not known about Gary Martin's demise, she would not suspect anything out of the norm. She did not know what she expected to see. Blood on the floor? Some energetic residue of a trauma? There was nothing except a furry little body shaking in her arms.

Unaware of the private trauma happening in front of her, Maureen showed Autumn through the open and spotless first floor complete with furniture. As they moved away from the foyer, Chrissy calmed down but Autumn continued to hold her.

"The house is being sold with everything in it."

"I'm surprised that the house went on the market so quickly. How did you get it ready so fast?"

"Gary Martin's sister called me the day she got the news her brother had died. The will gave her authority to do so."

"Did she sound upset?"

"When his sister, Anna, called me to list the house, she sounded like she accepted the death, almost as though she wasn't surprised."

"Hmm. What about his parents?"

"I haven't spoken to them. Seems Anna was the only one mentioned in his will. Probably thought he'd outlive his parents and she would be the only one left. I believe she's his younger sister."

"It seems kind of cold to me."

"To each his own. I'm just glad they called me to list the property. Once the police tape came down, I had the whole place cleaned and ready in one day. There was no clutter, so it was easy. All we had to do was remove Gary's personal items and his sister came to pick them up. The police left a bit of a mess, but it was no big deal to get the scuff marks off the marble."

An ornately carved oak bar stood in the corner of the living room. Autumn could picture it stocked with top-shelf liquor and ready for a party. The décor gave her some insight into Gary's expensive, sophisticated taste. She wondered if a decorator had helped him. The bachelors she knew lived in man caves, decorated for function rather than aesthetics.

They mounted the steps to the second floor. Maureen led them down the span of thick cream carpeting toward a double-doored entryway into the ordered master suite. Chrissy mewled. Anger welled in Autumn's chest at the person who caused Chrissy such heartache. She would do everything possible to bring them to justice.

"Another minute, sweetheart, and we'll be out of here," Autumn murmured in Chrissy's ear.

Autumn made a quick visit to the master bathroom and looked inside the medicine cabinet. Clean. Again, she was not sure what she expected to find. An obvious stash of fentanyl? She did not even know what that would look like and vowed to do some research when they got home.

She decided Chrissy had had enough and went back downstairs and out the front door. Once outside, Chrissy calmed down, so Autumn let her onto the pavement. She smiled at seeing Chrissy use the technique of feeling her feet on the ground.

"The place is in great condition," said Autumn.

"Move-in condition."

"Any idea how the person who found him got into the house, Maureen?"

"Rumor has it that the front door was open. Who knows if that's true?"

"You know, don't you," Autumn whispered to Chrissy, wishing that dogs could talk.

"Excuse me?"

"Nothing. Just calming Chrissy. Thanks for your time, Maureen."

"It was great seeing you. I'm at your service if you decide to buy or sell! Let's have lunch sometime soon."

"I'll be in touch."

Autumn waved as they pulled out of the driveway. Her thoughts turned to Gary's sister, Anna, wanting to know more about her. Anyone who could turn down Chrissy knowing she would wind up in the shelter seemed cold-hearted.

Back home, Autumn went outside with Chrissy to let her smell the plants and the ground to shake off the difficult visit to her former home. Seeing the house gave her a better idea of Gary Martin, the space reflecting his luxury taste and Maureen providing information about his disaffected family. She decided to contact Anna Martin.

She sipped some ice water and let Chrissy back in while waiting for her computer to boot up. The sound of Chrissy lapping up water made Autumn smile.

Autumn's Internet search for Anna Martin proved successful. It was scary how much personal information was available online. Anna's relatives, including Gary, age, addresses, and phone number showed up with a few clicks of the keyboard. She dialed the number listed. A woman answered on the third ring.

"Hello?"

"Hi, my name is Autumn Clarke. I'd like to speak with Anna Martin."

"I'm Anna. Do I know you?"

"No. I adopted Chrissy, Gary's Shih Tzu."

"So how did you get my number?"

"Online."

"What do you want?"

"Just trying to get information about Chrissy. Can you share what you know about her?"

"I'm not an animal person, so I didn't pay much attention to her. I told the cops to pack up her stuff and take her to the shelter."

Autumn boiled at the thought.

"It must have taken quite a while to find everything. She had a lot of toys and things."

"Gary was an idiot when it came to that dog. He spent way too much money on her and not enough on us."

"I'll probably be guilty of the same thing."

Autumn's half-joke did not get a response.

"Anyway, I wanted you to know that Chrissy is safe and in a loving home."

"Well, now I know."

Click.

"Hello?"

Nothing.

Autumn wondered if Anna was aware of the investigation. That bit of information might have taken her off guard. She turned to Chrissy who sat in her chair, looking out the window.

"You're better off with me, sweetheart."

Chrissy met her gaze, smiled, and wagged her tail.

That avenue closed, Autumn did a Google search on fentanyl. It brought up thousands of hits, including several news stories about accidental overdoses by users and law enforcement personnel. One link told of a police officer who experienced a near overdose and almost died from brushing some fentanyl powder from his uniform during a drug bust. The effect was immediate. Four injections of an antidote helped him regain consciousness. Weeks later, he still suffered from the effects of the drug, including drowsiness, nausea, and confusion. The thought of Ray encountering the drug in the course of his work worried her. The detective entered her mind at every opportunity. It took her off guard in a good way.

Information about the commercial version of the drug was available on pharmaceutical websites. She discovered that fentanyl is a powerful synthetic opioid similar to morphine but fifty to one hundred times more potent. Because of its high potential for abuse, it is a restricted drug typically used to treat patients with severe pain or to manage pain after surgery. Autumn wondered what her neighbor, Steve, was taking for his post-surgical pain. She made a note of the prescription names for the drug.

She went on to read that the prescription form of fentanyl is well controlled and administered to patients via injection, transdermal patch to be absorbed through the skin, or in lozenges. Non-pharmaceutical fentanyl cooked up in illegal labs and distributed as a powder, spiked on blotter paper, mixed with or substituted for heroin, or as tablets accounted for the majority of overdoses. Gary could swallow, snort, or inject fentanyl, or take it orally on blotter paper and have it absorbed through the mucous membrane.

According to her research, the fast-acting compound takes effect right away. He could have taken it at any time before his death, but if that were the case, the question remained as to why he died in the foyer and not somewhere else. Which brought Autumn back to the notion that Gary encountered the drug, or someone who administered the drug, upon entering his home.

Autumn found that death from fentanyl was due to respiratory depression and arrest. Therefore, it was possible that Gary suffocated rather than having had a heart attack. How did the drug get into his system? Where did he get it? Did he purchase it himself? The questions churned and ideas of how to find the answers began to click in.

≈8≈

Anna stood, arm limp, cordless phone still in hand. Her body shook with anger. How dare this woman call her? She was sick of the questions. The constant barrage of people connected to Gary who reached out to console, question, and deliver information. She knew more about her brother now than when he was alive.

"Who was it, dear?"

"No one to worry about, Mom."

But was she? She had been careless with Gary's cell phone, and now it was in the hands of the police. She finished preparing iced tea and sandwiches for her parents and set it on the cocktail table in the living room. Their favorite shows were on, eyes glued to the television set, a temporary reprieve from grief over the loss of their beloved son. If she had died rather than Gary, they would not be mourning to this degree.

Gary never bothered much with them or with her. He claimed that he was always working. His monetary contributions came when she requested them, but it was never enough to support her parents and her drug habit. The pain medication prescribed after her accident cost a bundle. Her injuries forced her out of waitressing and back into her parents' house. The disability payments were minimal. Now she had Gary's money at her disposal. When the house sold, it would be even better.

She sat at the kitchen table and sipped hot coffee. It was seventy degrees outside, but the call about Chrissy had chilled her. The dog and the cell phone were loose ends that she could do nothing about at this point. She balled her fists. Gary persisted in her life even in death.

=9=

Autumn had been preparing for lunch with Julie and her friend all morning. When the doorbell rang, Chrissy sounded the alert, barking to announce that they had company. As Autumn opened the door for her guests, Teddy entered first and ran over to Chrissy. Their greeting commenced in a flurry of wagging tails, hopping motions, and little squeals. Julie came next, followed by her friend, Francesca Barnes, the legal assistant, but most people called her Fran. Julie wore her signature floral top and colorful clam diggers, while Fran's white slacks and striped knit short-sleeved top had spring written all over it. Autumn's own casual look of jeans and pink cotton T-shirt matched Chrissy's pink satin hair ribbons.

"Autumn, this is Fran Barnes."

"Nice to meet you, Fran. Please come in."

Fran spotted Chrissy and squatted down, holding out her arms. "Chrissy!"

The call interrupted Chrissy's interactions with Teddy. She stopped, turned, and ran over to Fran. The woman rubbed Chrissy and spoke to her with familiarity. Chrissy's excitement made Autumn feel a little curious about their relationship, but glad she had something positive from her old life to connect with. Chrissy flipped over to give Fran her tummy.

"So good to see you!" Fran rubbed Chrissy's belly with gusto. "You look beautiful! Someone is taking good care of you."

The acknowledgment made Autumn smile. Fran stood up and Chrissy returned to entertaining Teddy by leading him over to the toy pile.

Autumn led her guests outside. At the sound of the sliding glass door opening, Chrissy and Teddy came rushing out, happy to play in the grass. The patio looked elegant. Lunch was set on a table with a white cloth amidst the potted annuals and the thriving perennials of purple, yellow, and white. The Knockout roses had blossomed with bright pink flowers seemingly overnight. Water bowls and snack plates for the pups occupied a spot nearby on separate placemats.

Autumn noticed that Chrissy had retrieved a ball from the pile and brought it to where they romped. The women took their seats at the wrought iron table and chairs with high ornate backs and thick tufted cushions. A vase filled with peonies from the yard completed the lovely set-up. Autumn poured unsweetened iced tea into their glasses.

"Lunch is almost ready. I hope you like salmon."

"Sounds wonderful," said Julie. Autumn remembered it as one of Julie's favorite meals.

"Fran, thanks so much for coming today."

"No problem. I couldn't resist a chance to see Chrissy...and to meet you, of course."

"Of course," Autumn smiled at playing second fiddle to a charismatic Shih Tzu. "She loves you!"

"Gary brought her to the office quite often. He didn't like her to be alone, and he could leave her with us when he had court."

"Us?"

"Our office has two legal assistants, including me. The practice is busy. We could've used one more person before, but now..."

"Yes, so sad," said Julie.

"The news broke my heart."

"Were you close?" asked Autumn, taking a sip of tea.

"As close as any co-workers become. We spent eight or more hours a day together. Gary was a great guy."

"How so?" Autumn wondered about this woman's relationship with Gary.

"How he always remembered birthdays. The way he cared for Chrissy."

"Well, Chrissy certainly misses her daddy."

Fran did not comment and took a sip of tea, wiping her hand on a napkin.

"What did he die from?"

"His sister told us he had a heart attack. Not surprising."

Julie ignored the false information and made no move to correct Fran. Autumn played dumb, as well.

"Do you know his sister well?" asked Autumn.

"Not especially. Why?"

"Just wondering why she allowed Chrissy to go to the shelter."

"No idea, but I can't imagine her taking care of Chrissy the way Gary would have wanted. The tone she used when delivering the news about Gary sounded as though she'd bought a dress on sale, not that her brother had passed. And she wouldn't answer any questions."

Fran took a sip of tea and continued.

"Lisa and I mothered him, making sure he took care of himself, which he didn't. I think the stress of the practice got to him."

"Lisa Coleman?"

53

"Yep. She's been there a little over a year. She took to Gary. How do you know her?"

"She's my neighbor's daughter. What do you mean 'she took to him'?"

"Acted like she was in love with him. Always said bad things about his girlfriends."

Autumn looked at her watch, making sure to check the salmon before it overcooked.

"I'll be right back with lunch."

She took the teriyaki salmon out of the oven and placed the filets atop mixed greens, shaved carrots, avocado, and sunflower seeds topped with a summer vinaigrette. Mom had bought the plates on sale and they were her dad's favorites for eating outside. Tears threatened and her hands shook. She wondered if she should take another dose of her medication, but instead waited a moment and refocused on preparing lunch. Her effort calmed the trembling. She grabbed two loaded plates and brought them outside.

"Here you go," said Autumn as she put the plates down next to the yellow cloth napkins wrapped around silverware.

"Marvelous!" said Julie.

Julie's excitement about food amused Autumn.

"Thank you, It looks delicious." said Fran.

Autumn retrieved her own serving along with a few snacks for Chrissy and Teddy, and came back outside. She spotted the furry children as they played ball in the middle of the yard. It made her happy that Teddy helped Chrissy get relief from her sorrow. She put the snacks on two little plates for when they were ready to indulge.

"Tell me more about Gary Martin."

"Very serious, always working, except when he took a break to play with Chrissy. She was his heart. No pun intended."

"Understandable. He worked on criminal cases?"

"Primarily, yes, but he also took on personal injury and civil suits."

"Any cases come to mind that were particularly stressful for Mr. Martin?"

"Stress does so much damage. People don't realize the consequences of a steady diet of tension. You can have physical symptoms, such as headaches, upset stomach, high blood pressure, chest pain, and problems with sex and sleep," said Julie.

She sounded like a medical journal.

"I don't think he had a problem with sex, given that he juggled two women. He complained about, but usually ignored, the rest."

Fran took a bite of salad and a sip of tea. She wiped her hand on the napkin to free it of the condensation from the glass. Robins chirped, providing a musical backdrop.

"Stress can also have emotional symptoms," said Julie.

"He appeared distracted. He let a plea deal expire, and that's not something he usually does, er, did."

"Sounds like a serious mistake," Autumn said between bites of salad.

"The client was livid. He threatened Gary. And this guy is a repeat drug offender. It scared me the day he came in the office and raised hell."

"Who?" Autumn tried to sound casual.

"People in the next office suite heard him and we filed a police report, so I guess it's a matter of public record. His name is Travis Mitchell."

Autumn made a mental note. With lunch consumed, she cleared the plates and served a strawberry shortcake. Julie's eyes widened.

"What a perfect end to our meal," Julie said through a big smile.

≈10≈

Twilight settled over the peaceful neighborhood as Autumn and Chrissy strolled down the sidewalk.

"Did you have fun with Teddy today?"

Chrissy looked at Autumn and wagged her tail.

"What a wonderful hostess you are."

Chrissy smiled up at her. There was no mistaking it this time. Autumn had grown used to Chrissy's expressions and accepted them as true. Chrissy let out her shrieking bark. The white mass up ahead proved to be Mickey accompanied by Steve.

"Ahoy there matey!" called Autumn.

"Ahoy!" shouted Steve.

Chrissy started straining at the leash, encouraging Autumn forward. They behaved as though it had been years instead of days since they had seen each other. Autumn wondered at a dog's sense of time.

"We're going for a quick one tonight. My daughter is here."

"I'd love to meet her sometime." Autumn had the afternoon luncheon conversation burning in her brain.

"Let's walk and then go to my house. She's dying to see Chrissy."

"I guess it's big news in the legal circles about Chrissy's adoption."

"She's very popular!"

They shared a laugh at Chrissy's magnetic personality and ambled around the block, making sure the furry friends hit all of their favorite spots. The journey came full circle at Steve's cozy ranch house with bursts of hot pink and white azaleas surrounding the front of the house. Autumn decided to wait to ask Steve about his medications.

"Come on in."

The smell of tomato sauce, garlic, and basil made Autumn hungry. Steve removed Mickey's leash and hung it on a hook in the closet. Autumn kept Chrissy on the leash since they did not plan to stay long.

They walked into the kitchen where Lisa stirred a pot filled with spaghetti. Her dark brown to blonde ombre hair cascaded over the shoulders of her turquoise blouse. Autumn wondered how much the dye job cost her. She considered getting highlights and wondered if Ray would like her hair better if it had more depth.

"Lisa, this is Autumn. And, of course, Chrissy."

Chrissy's tail wagged at Lisa.

"Sweetheart!" Lisa ran over to Chrissy and gave her a hug. "I missed you!" And to Autumn, "I would have adopted her if I had known she landed in the shelter. I assumed someone in Gary's family would take her. You lucked out."

"I certainly did," said Autumn.

"She's better off with you than with Gary's family anyway. His sister is self-absorbed and his parents are not in good health."

"You know his sister?"

"Mostly from how Gary talked about her. It surprised me that he left her everything."

"He told you that?"

"I witnessed his Last Will and Testament, along with Vaughn. I'd pick a charity over her. She always asked him for money. Now she's got it all."

"So she struggled financially?"

"Anna lived with their parents and blew money left and right. Gary said she had an addiction to oxy at one point. I can't figure out why he kept giving her money. Maybe for his parents. I'll bet if Chrissy had inherited the money, she would have taken her in." Lisa scowled at the thought.

Autumn decided to change the subject.

"I guess it's hard not seeing Chrissy at the office anymore."

"Definitely. She helped soften the stress in there. Hey, you should bring her by sometime."

"I'd love to. Name the day."

"Day after tomorrow. Everyone will be in, including Vaughn. Stop by in the morning."

"I will. I can say hello to Fran."

"Fran?"

"She's a friend of a friend. Met her earlier today."

Autumn caught a quick look of disgust as Lisa's mouth turned down at the corners then faded.

"Fran said the two of you mothered Gary and Chrissy."

"He depended on me the most. No one took care of him the way I did."

"What about his girlfriends?"

"He had more than one? Lucky SOB," said Steve.

Autumn smiled at his candor.

"They drove him nuts. Alexis Davenport and Miranda Green both. Then it got worse."

"What happened?"

"They accidentally ran into each other at Elegant Nails salon and had a brawl in the middle of the room."

"Maybe he wasn't so lucky after all," said Steve.

"They both wanted to marry him. He told me that he didn't want either of them." She gave the pasta a stir.

Chrissy paced back and forth and looked at Autumn.

"Listen, I need to get Chrissy fed, so I'll see you in a couple of days. See you later, Steve."

"See ya."

Mickey walked them to the door.

Chrissy and Autumn were home in a few minutes, and Autumn got her settled, removing her leash and harness.

"What was that about?"

Chrissy sat and looked at her.

"You hungry?"

Chrissy licked her lips.

"Okay, let's make you a delicious dinner."

Watching Chrissy eat without having to coax her lifted Autumn's mood. They were making progress. With less worry about Chrissy's day-to-day routine, Autumn focused on the mystery of her pet parent's death. She sat at the kitchen table and made a list of people connected to Gary Martin, planning her strategy to meet them all.

=11=

As promised, Autumn brought Chrissy around to the law office of Martin and Evans. The small lobby area accommodated three doors and a clearly marked suite, the name of the firm engraved on a brass sign. The odor of artificial lemon commercial floor cleaner permeated the space.

She opened the door. Lisa and Fran sat near the entrance behind wood desks piled with file folders and papers. The bright landscape art hung on tan walls took emphasis away from the industrial gray and tan carpet.

"Chrissy!" they exclaimed in unison, jumping from their chairs to greet the sweet pup. Chrissy's tail wagged at the attention.

"What's all the commotion?" Vaughn Evans said as he emerged from his office. "Hey, Chrissy!"

At just under six feet tall with salt and pepper hair and a bright white smile, Autumn could see him winning over a jury. He was as bad as the girls were when it came to this fuzzy diva. She had a way with people. Autumn extended her hand to Vaughn.

"I'm Autumn Clarke, Chrissy's new mommy."

"What a lucky dog!" he said shaking Autumn's hand and ruffling Chrissy's mane. His eyes did a not-so-subtle assessment of Autumn's figure.

"Lisa's dad is my neighbor."

"Well, sounds like it's all in the family."

"Do you have a few minutes? I'd like to speak with you about a personal matter."

"Sure, right this way."

Autumn and Chrissy followed Vaughn into his office. The ladies let out an audible sigh at Chrissy's departure and returned to work.

Vaughn pointed to a gray upholstered chair for Autumn and took his place in the black leather executive chair behind the massive mahogany desk. Autumn could see his reflection on the surface. Chrissy curled up on the floor next to Autumn.

"What can I do for you?"

"It's more about Chrissy than myself. She's been through a lot, and I'm trying to find out more about her daddy to help me understand her better. Can you fill me in?"

Vaughn picked up a Montblanc pen and twirled it.

"Gary was high-strung. A perfectionist. He worked hard and partied harder."

"His house is on the market. I saw it online." Autumn thought it best to withhold her visit to Gary's home.

"That monstrosity. Why a single guy would want such a big house is beyond me."

"Must have cost a fortune."

"It did. He had to work three times as hard just to support the place, along with his extra-curricular activities."

"I'm curious as to what you think about his death. Is it possible that he did drugs?"

Vaughn paused a few beats, his eyes shifted down to his desk and back up to meet Autumn's.

"Maybe recreational, but nothing serious. I'm sure it was a heart attack." His matter-of-fact tone had a hint of dismissal.

Autumn changed tactics.

"I guess being an attorney is stressful."

"You have no idea. We deal with constant conflict and Gary had some nutty clients."

"Like Travis Mitchell?"

"News travels fast. He's a good example of a nutcase. Drug dealer. Threatened Gary right here in the office. We no longer represent him."

"Is it possible Travis may have harmed Gary?"

"Anything is possible. There's another guy, Dean Sanders, who took to stalking Gary to convince him to represent him. Like I said, nuts. Made Gary paranoid."

"How come?"

"Sanders was unstable. Got a hold of Gary's cell phone number and harassed him on a regular basis."

"Could Sanders have a reason to harm Gary?"

"Doubt it. There was no sign of violence when they found him, so it must have been his heart."

She looked down at Chrissy.

"Lisa said Gary had two girlfriends. What about them?"

"He spent money like water and bought them all kinds of things to keep them happy. He lived beyond his means and constantly chased the almighty dollar. His theory was to keep a high-end outward appearance so our clients thought he won all of his cases."

"And did he?"

"He won more than he lost, but he still didn't have enough to maintain the house, his expensive wardrobe, the women, and the Porsche."

"And his sister?" said Autumn.

"She called him every week, saying she needed money to support their parents. He couldn't say no."

"On top of all the other expenses."

"He was stretched to the limit," said Vaughn.

"That's some heavy stress on top of the day-to-day attorney stressors."

"We all told him to take better care of himself. Brilliant attorney, but made his own trouble."

"Do you think his stress had an effect on Chrissy?"

"Wouldn't be surprised. In my experience, dogs absorb whatever is going on with their owners."

Autumn thought about that and realized that her own issues could have a negative impact on Chrissy. She resolved to double her efforts to overcome her trauma for her own sake as well as Chrissy's.

"What did he do to relax?"

"Used scotch as a stress reducer. Said that took care of it." He shook his head. "What a waste."

Autumn looked at Chrissy who sensed her attention and looked up. Autumn reached down to pet her.

"Is there anything else you can tell me about Chrissy and Gary?"

"She was the one thing in his life that kept him happy. Without her, he probably wouldn't have lasted as long as he did."

Chrissy beat her tail on the floor, seeming to understand she was a good influence on Gary Martin. Autumn stood up and thanked Vaughn for his time. She and Chrissy made their way past Fran and Lisa in a flurry of sweet goodbyes to Chrissy.

That was twice the girlfriends had come up, as well as Anna Martin. Travis Mitchell was confirmed as a troublemaker. A new player, Dean Sanders, was introduced into the mix. Autumn needed to find out more about them.

≈12≈

Knollwood's dog park was a popular hangout for dogs of all breeds and sizes. Pet parents lounged on the freshly painted green benches while their furry children romped in the fenced area. Some complained that there should be separation from large and small dogs, but the township ignored them.

Autumn entered through the first gate and closed it behind her, and then entered through the main gate into the grass and woodchip-laden play zone. The double-gated system was the best way to keep the dogs from accidentally exiting the fenced area.

"Have fun, sweetheart."

She let Chrissy off the leash. Happy barking sounds drew Chrissy into the group of about ten pets. The smell of mowed grass hit the bridge of Autumn's nose. She wiggled it and sniffed to avoid sneezing.

Autumn saw Chrissy run toward a large German shepherd dog at the far end of the field. They wagged their tails and Autumn frowned, keeping an eye on her little one in case the larger dog wanted to get rough.

"Don't worry, Ace won't hurt her."

Autumn looked over to see Detective Ray Reed centered on the bench, his arms outstretched across the back, legs crossed in a casual posture. He looked even better in a form-fitting white T-shirt and jeans than he did in a suit.

"Oh! I didn't even see you there. It's like you read my mind about Chrissy playing with a bigger dog. I thought he looked familiar."

"Nice to see you. Have a seat."

Ray slid over and patted the spot next to him while looking over at Ace. She appreciated that he tried to make her feel comfortable around him. She sat, her eyes focused on Chrissy to avoid staring at Ray's muscular chest and arms.

"Freshly mowed grass gets to me sometimes, too."

Autumn smiled and blushed, realizing he had noticed her since she arrived. She rubbed her nose and hoped her allergies did not kick in.

"It's nice they've become friends," said Autumn, hoping to change the subject.

"Yeah, they met at Gary Martin's when we were called to the scene."

"Why didn't you tell me before? Withholding information, Detective?"

Ray laughed at Autumn's attempt to sound official. Autumn liked the sound of his laughter. It felt like sunshine warming her heart.

"It didn't seem pertinent at the time."

Autumn smiled. "Either way, it's nice that Chrissy has a friend who can protect her if any of these dogs makes a threat."

"So do you."

Autumn's eyebrows went up, hoping Ray meant that he was there for her, but she did not push and he did not elaborate.

"Speaking of Gary Martin…"

"Were we?"

Autumn let out a frustrated sigh. Ray smirked and folded his hands in his lap.

"Did you find anything interesting about the case?"

"One or two things could be helpful. I'm looking into it."

"Well, if you promise to keep me updated, I have some new information that might interest you."

"Snooping around, eh?"

Autumn looked down before continuing. Something about Ray's boyish good looks and intense gaze brought out her awkward side. She had had the same experience in her romance with Scott Bancroft five years ago. It ended with months of crying and low self-esteem at being dumped for a newer model. Her mother had offered to take her on a cruise to forget about him, but Autumn refused. She often wished she had gone, if for no other reason than to spend time with her parents.

"How about an informant relationship? You tell me things. I tell you things. I won't even charge you."

"I'll show you mine if you show me yours?"

Her cheeks were burning hot at the innuendo. Ray chuckled.

"Sorry. Didn't mean to embarrass you."

Autumn ached to change the subject. She cleared her throat. Her gaze wandered over to where Chrissy and Ace were chasing each other.

"I've started digging into Chrissy's life before she came to live with me."

"Understandable, wanting to find out more about Chrissy."

"I met Gary's secretaries and his business partner."

"You've been busy."

Autumn crossed her arms in a defensive posture.

"Are you interested or not?"

Ray bent his elbows and held up his hands in surrender, muscles bulging under the short-sleeved T-shirt. She had never considered arms as sexy. She got a hold of herself and nodded her head in triumph before continuing.

"Gary Martin's death was due to a drug overdose, but I have a strong sense that it wasn't his own doing."

Autumn left out the part about where she learned of the overdose.

"Those kinds of instinctive feelings are important to follow-up on, but you should let me do it."

Autumn glared at him. He closed his mouth and waved his hand for her to continue.

"Vaughn Evans, Gary's partner, said Gary was living beyond his means. Maybe he owed someone money and they killed him over it. Lisa Coleman, one of his legal assistants, said Gary's girlfriends didn't care about him the way she did, but fought over who would get him. Fran Barnes, the other assistant, said Lisa had a crush on him."

She waited to see Ray's reaction, but he maintained a poker face.

"And?"

Autumn waited a beat before continuing.

"If Gary was doing drugs, he wouldn't have been doing them the moment he walked through the door." Autumn flipped one hand, palm up. "Right?" She could see Ray's wheels were turning to process this new information.

"Are you familiar with the behavior of addicts, Ms. Clarke?" Ray said with mock formality.

"If you must know, my mother did fundraising for the treatment of drug abuse and addiction in Bucks County, so I have some understanding of the topic. Also, a client of Gary's, Travis Mitchell, who happens to be a drug dealer, threatened him after he screwed up a plea bargain."

"What makes you think I haven't already followed up on these leads?"

Undaunted, Autumn persisted.

"And another potential client was stalking and harassing him. Dean Sanders."

"Did he say why?"

"Gary refused to represent him."

Ray took out a small pad and pen and wrote down the name.

"Does this mean you'll check into these suspects?"

"I'll check on Dean Sanders. We've already spoken to the others. I wonder why neither Vaughn nor the secretaries had mentioned Sanders when I interviewed them."

"You're looking for motives, right? Isn't it usually someone closest to the victim?"

"You watch too much television, Autumn." His brilliant white smile and the use of her first name took Autumn off-guard. She looked away.

"Even so, what about Gary's sister, Anna? She was the only one who benefits from his death."

"I'm not at liberty to discuss her. No offense."

Growing impatient, Autumn turned away.

"By the way, I wanted to tell you how sorry I am about your parents."

"Thanks. How did you know?"

"I did a little checking on you."

Autumn pushed her feet into the ground and looked at him square in the eyes.

"You did? And why in heaven's name would you do that, Detective?"

"Curiosity, mostly. I like to know who I'm dealing with."

A little pang of disappointment hit Autumn.

"The accident is why I got Chrissy. She helps me."

"Dogs are the most stable friends you can have. I don't know what I would have done without Ace. He keeps me sane both on the job and at home. From what I've seen in my line of work, it's hard to trust people. Ace is good company, and I rely on him."

On cue, Chrissy and Ace came running up, tongues hanging out. Autumn opened her travel bag and pulled out portable water bowls. George Clarke hit home the lesson of being prepared, so she had two bowls in case the first one cracked. Waving off Ray's offer of using his bottle of water, she filled both bowls using her supply. The furry friends enthusiastically lapped the cool water. Their smiles and dripping faces made Autumn glad she had plenty for both of them. Ray's smile made her heart sing. The pups ran off toward the rest of the pack.

"We've only been together a little under two weeks. She's the best thing I could have hoped for."

Ray glanced over at Ace and Chrissy playing in the grass and nodded. Even though her comfort level with Ray increased as they talked, Autumn decided not tell him about her post-traumatic stress symptoms just yet. She did not want him to think she was unstable.

"There's a place where they have outdoor seating and allow dogs. Want to grab a bite when they're finished?"

"Hmm. You're basically a stranger, and I didn't have the same advantages you did of doing a background check, Detective." Autumn gave him a sideway glance and a smart-aleck grin.

He smiled. "Call me Ray. Follow me to the café so I can't kidnap you."

Autumn began to relax and chuckled.

"Deal."

The Corner Café's yellow and green striped awnings brightened the brick building, making it easy to find in the middle of Main Street. Ray exited his vehicle. Autumn crept into a parking space. She was gentle with Chrissy as she took her out of the car seat.

"Afraid of getting a ticket?"

"What? Oh, no. I'm a stickler for the speed limit."

"Most people don't seem to care."

"I'm all about safety," Autumn battled to keep her focus on Ray and not allow her mind to wander to the accident.

The server seated them and they placed their orders for the four of them. Ace and Chrissy sat under the table, enjoying bowls of water and eating hamburgers without the bun after their hard day of frolicking. Autumn and Ray were relieved to be in the shade of a large patio umbrella and sipped raspberry iced teas that were perfect with their tuna-on-whole-wheat sandwiches.

"I've been here a few times and never noticed that they allow dogs," said Autumn.

"It's funny what you discover when you have a dog. The world seems to revolve around them."

Autumn took a sip of tea. It seemed natural to be here with Ray, Ace, and Chrissy. It was a shame that it took a death to bring them all together.

"The energy at Gary Martin's office is strange," said Autumn.

"The energy? What do you mean?"

"Like there's a rehearsed set of information the secretaries and his partner give to people who question them. Something is off."

A slight breeze cooled them, bringing with it the aroma of French fries.

"Well, they told you more than they told me. I wasn't privileged to the fact that Lisa had a crush on him or that she hated his girlfriends. I should let you question all of my female suspects."

She could imagine working with Ray late into the night, sitting on her living room sofa going over clues with the pups lounging nearby.

"So they are suspects?"

"Not at this point, but I admit we're at a standstill. You bring up a good point about the drug. How did it get in his system? And how did you find out about it?"

"A good investigator never reveals her sources."

"Yeah, well your investigation isn't sanctioned by me or the department." He used air quotes around the word *investigation*.

Autumn pressed her lips together. She was not going to let Ray or anyone else stop her from finding out who murdered Chrissy's daddy. She took a deep breath and continued.

"Vaughn Evans was open about Gary's lifestyle and work habits but insisted it was a stress-induced heart attack. The women came across as protective."

Ray dropped his scolding and continued in a more cooperative tone.

"Maybe it's worthwhile to talk to Mr. Evans again."

Autumn nodded her agreement.

"There could be other clients besides Travis Mitchell and Dean Sanders who had it in for Gary Martin."

"We'll see."

"Another person of interest is Gary's sister, Anna. She inherited his entire estate."

"I'm open to reaffirming her alibi," said Ray.

"So she is a suspect!"

"I didn't say that. We talk to everyone who is close to the victim. Standard procedure."

Autumn pouted.

"Is that cute look of yours how you weasel information from your sources?"

She flushed, and Ray smiled.

"Should I keep you informed if I find out anything else?

Ray gave her his cell number.

"I'd rather you stayed out of it, but I doubt you will. Use it in case you find out anything of interest...or get into trouble."

Ray's intense gaze warned her to be careful. Autumn realized he was right.

≈13≈

Ray got out of his unmarked vehicle and attached Ace's leash before leading him out of the hatch. His mind turned to Autumn and her persistence. Her perspective made him want to push Vaughn a little harder. He smiled, thinking of how she became a little shy around him. The trait endeared her to him.

He pushed open the office door. Fran and Lisa looked up from their computers.

"Hi, Detective. How can we help you?" said Fran.

Ray detected a note of annoyance in Fran's tone.

"I'm here to see Mr. Evans. Is he available?"

Fran picked up the phone and dialed Vaughn's extension.

"Detective Reed is here, Vaughn." She nodded and hung up.

"You can go right in." She pointed to the hallway.

Ray gave a courtesy knock and walked in without waiting for a reply. Vaughn sat at his executive desk and continued to work.

Without looking up, Vaughn spoke. "Take a seat, Detective."

Ray chose the upholstered guest chair to the right of the desk closest to the window. After a few more beats, Vaughn made eye contact.

"Now, what can I do for you?"

"Tell me about your relationship with Gary Martin."

"Haven't we been through this already?"

Ray did not like Vaughn's attitude, arrogance, and disrespect.

"Let's go over it again."

"Gary was a brilliant attorney. I was lucky to have him as my partner."

"What about your personal relationship?"

"We didn't get together outside the office. We had very differently lifestyles."

"How do you mean?"

"Gary liked the ladies and the nightlife. I prefer to read a book and have a quiet evening at home."

"Did his partying affect the business?"

Vaughn hesitated.

"He missed at least one deadline for a plea bargain for Travis Mitchell, which is why the man came in here raising hell. Can't blame him. And…"

Vaughn took a breath, reluctant to continue. His hands balled into fists.

Ray waited.

"And there are funds missing from our accounts."

This was new information. Ray's interest piqued.

"How much?"

"Almost three hundred thousand dollars."

Ray whistled. Quite a sum to go missing.

"Why didn't you mention this before, Mr. Evans?"

"That would be considered motive, and I didn't want the hassle."

"So you're sure Mr. Martin took it?"

"I'm not sure of anything. We fought about it."

"How did you discover the discrepancy?"

"By accident. The accountant and I reviewed the attorney trust account and noticed the balance showed less money than the settlement checks we received. There was also a discrepancy in the business account."

"Who had access to the accounts?"

"Besides Gary and me, our accountant did, and our legal assistants, as well."

Ray made a note.

"What happened when you confronted Mr. Martin about the missing money?"

"He denied it. We argued."

"Could it have been one of your assistants?"

"They make deposits and such, but the bleeding stopped once Gary died."

"Did Gary Martin take drugs?"

"Gary drank scotch, and may have used drugs for recreational purposes, but not as a habit as far as I know."

"For the record, do you have an alibi for the evening of Mr. Martin's death?"

"Like I said before, I spent a quiet evening at home."

"Is there anyone who can vouch for you being at home?"

"I live alone."

"What about Dean Sanders? I understand he stalked Gary Martin."

Vaughn tipped his head to the side, giving the detective a sideways glance.

"Where did you hear that, Detective?"

Ray ignored the question. Vaughn continued.

"He did. We chose not to represent him because he seemed delusional. Couldn't tell if he was telling the truth or making up stories. Then Sanders persisted and made Gary uncomfortable. He seemed harmless to me."

Ray made a note next to Dean Sanders' name.

"You didn't mention him before."

"Didn't think it pertinent."

"Please just share what you know. I'll determine what's relevant. One last thing. I'd like contact information for your accountant."

Vaughn called Fran on the intercom and told her to provide Detective Reed with their accountant's information.

Ray walked out of Vaughn's office, his mood grim. He grabbed the note with the accountant's name, number, and address and left under the watchful eyes of Fran and Lisa. Autumn was right. This place had a weird vibe. Like everyone was hiding something.

◦14◦

Vaughn's mind churned, as did his stomach. Detective Reed's questions took him off guard. The only person he'd discussed Dean Sanders with was Autumn Clarke. She must have told Reed. He could not remember why he'd even brought Sanders up in the first place. It was her relaxed demeanor and sweet countenance that let his guard down. Besides, he always liked Chrissy and was happy she had found a good home.

He did not expect a connection between Autumn Clarke and Detective Reed. What had she told him? It may work in his favor, but it could also hurt him in the end. Dean Sanders was a weasel and could not be trusted. Throwing suspicion in his direction could backfire on Vaughn. The accountant would provide evidence of the missing money, but he could not trace it to a particular person.

Vaughn leaned back in the imposing executive chair. Since Gary died, Vaughn's power trickled away from fear of exposure and a doubled workload. He missed his partner to some degree but did not miss the arguments about money and women. Gary was too righteous for his own good. He also wasted money and made stupid mistakes that could have cost them their reputation.

Vaughn's personal and professional image was still on the line. Worry about the missing money and Detective Reed's inquiry obliterated his concentration. He rubbed his temples. He needed a better plan. Vaughn pushed away from his desk and left the office without a word to Fran and Lisa.

≈15≈

The women watched Vaughn stride out of the office. They were familiar with his moods and did not ask questions about when he would be back or where he was going. Fran was expert at deflecting clients who demanded to know when Vaughn could speak with them. As the door clicked shut, they looked at each other.

"What's going on?" said Lisa.

"Nothing that I'm aware of," said Fran.

"I wonder if it has to do with Detective Reed."

"He doesn't like Reed, that's for sure. He complained last time the detective was here."

Fran turned to continue her work.

"He's been on edge since Gary died."

"Let me worry about Vaughn."

"I still care about this practice."

"With Gary gone, there's a good chance you might be, too."

Lisa hated it when Fran growled at her.

"For now, you're stuck with me."

"Lucky me."

Lisa sighed. She was sick of the tension. She grabbed her purse and walked out.

Fran watched the door close, glad for the solitude. She wondered how much Gary's death created a strain on Vaughn. Their arguments over the last few weeks had escalated. With Gary no longer here, that part ended, but Vaughn seemed even antsier than before. Whatever it was, she would help him through it without Lisa's involvement.

⸗16⸗

Chrissy and Autumn sat side-by-side on the living room sofa. The elaborate Karistan rug and tiffany-style lamp provided a cozy atmosphere. The brain fog lifted enough to get some work done. Her research about the latest corporate assault on the environment itched to get out. Her right hand left the keyboard periodically to pet Chrissy who lounged next to her.

Her lunch with Ray kept popping into her mind. It gave her hope that, one, Ray would call her if he learned something about the case, and two, that he would call her because he just wanted to say hello. The idea made Autumn's stomach churn. Was she ready to get close to him? It might even hurt her chances of recovery if something happened that took her off center. She needed to consult Stephanie Douglas about Ray as soon as possible. She knew the most about Autumn's dating history and had her best interest at heart.

Autumn's interactions with Ray made her realize that she had not addressed all of the issues about her relationship with Scott. Ray's handsome face and the way he treated his dog with love and respect drew her to him. Still, getting involved with someone was not on her list of good moves. A romance was not the same as loving her pup.

Chrissy looked at her as though recognizing Autumn's thoughts. An unexpected wave of nausea came over Autumn and a flash of a scene, almost like a video, played before her eyes. The odd perspective came from much lower than Autumn's height. The visual shift made her dizzy. Suddenly, Ace's face loomed, panting. She was looking up at him, his nose wet, his tongue dripping. The vision halted. The dizziness and nausea subsided, but it took a minute to adjust to normal perception. Autumn looked at Chrissy who gave her a knowing smile.

"Did you do that?"

Chrissy pounded her tail on the sofa cushion and grunted. Autumn's jaw dropped. Could this be another possible hallucination? If it was not, Autumn had a telepathic fuzz ball on her hands. Chrissy's eyes glittered and she licked Autumn's hand then nodded and grunted again.

"You've been holding out on me, little one."

Autumn was amazed, a little shaken up, and flooded with thoughts about how Chrissy's ability could help her solve this case.

"You like Ace, don't you?"

Chrissy let out a loud, single bark.

"I like him too."

Chrissy's vision opened Autumn's mind to having Ace and Ray in their lives.

"Show me your daddy. Show me what you saw on his last night."

Chrissy's mouth closed and her gaze became intense. The discomfort, like motion sickness came over Autumn as she received the vision. She struggled to focus on the movie playing in her mind rather than on the need to run to the bathroom.

Gary Martin lifted Chrissy from the car. She wore no harness or leash. Autumn experienced his love for her as he cradled her, kissed her ear, and then tucked her under his arm, his big left hand comfortably supporting her belly and chest. She watched at eye level with the doorknob as he took a key out of his pocket, worked it in the lock, and grabbed the gold-toned handle. He turned it and walked inside, placing Chrissy on the foyer floor. Autumn viewed the inside of the house through Chrissy's eyes, from closer to the floor.

Chrissy looked up at her daddy who stood towering above her, texting on his cell phone. Sweat glistened on his face as he bit his lower lip. He hit send. His breathing labored, he sat down hard on the marble tile. He gave Chrissy a panicked look through the frown lines on his forehead. Autumn saw him strain to breathe and clutched his chest with his right hand as he fell over on his side. No one else appeared in the entryway. The sense of snuggling against Gary's left side faded with the vision, and so did her urge to vomit.

"You poor dear." She reached for Chrissy and held her close, kissing her soft head, tears in her eyes. "How terrible for you."

She rocked Chrissy, losing all sense of time, Chrissy's sorrow and her own sadness and pain melding. After a while, Chrissy wiggled in her arms and Autumn put her on the floor, Chrissy's body hot from being held so close.

"Can you show me more?"

Chrissy let out one loud bark.

"Okay, but we'll wait awhile. We both need a break. Let's go for a walk!"

Autumn affixed the harness and the leash and off they went down their street, the sidewalk providing a solid reality both of them needed. As they passed Steve Coleman's house, Chrissy turned and walked up the front path, fully expecting Autumn to follow. Mickey barked inside the house in response to their knock, and Chrissy returned the bark until Steve answered the door.

"Up for a walk?"

The four of them ambled up the street with Chrissy and Mickey leading the way.

"It was nice meeting Lisa. I didn't know her in school since we're ten years apart."

"I'm lucky that with her social life and schedule that she still makes time for the old man."

Autumn envied that Lisa had the opportunity to take care of her dad.

"How was your pasta the other night?"

"Pretty good. My daughter cooks well, but nothing like her mother."

"Smelled good to me."

"I think I just miss my wife puttering in the kitchen. Lisa can hold her own on a stove."

"I'm willing to put in my two cents if I get invited to dinner."

"Sure. I'll talk to Lisa about it."

"Great!" Autumn wanted to try her cooking and get more information about Gary Martin.

"She became agitated after you left. She didn't seem in the mood to talk and left after she cleaned up the dinner dishes."

"Maybe seeing Chrissy brought back memories of Gary and she got upset. Been there done that."

"Could be. It's still pretty fresh. She's worried about getting laid off with only one attorney in the office."

"Vaughn doesn't plan to replace Gary?"

"She's not sure, but Fran is Vaughn's primary legal assistant and Lisa was assigned to Gary. Things are up in the air right now."

"Nothing is certain these days. Taking it one day at a time is the best way to get through."

Dr. Wes's wisdom shot into her mind, telling her to stay in the moment and not anticipate things too far in advance. It worked as long as she caught her thoughts before they turned back in time to the accident and happy times that made her miss her parents. She caught the second half of what Steve was saying.

"...there used to be stability in the job market. No more."

Autumn nodded. Self-employment was her best option with the uncertainty of how her symptoms plagued her from one day to the next. She had grown used to working at home and preferred it. The flexible schedule allowed her to attend appointments with Dr. Wes, or to deal with panic attacks. A regular job would not work for her at this point; probably never. Besides, the substantial inheritance made work a choice rather than a necessity.

She tried to focus on what Steve was saying, but her thoughts flashed between Ray, the visions Chrissy showed her, and the list of suspects.

"...take her to the groomer?"

"Groomer?"

"Yeah, are you planning to get Chrissy a groomer?"

"I've been brushing and bathing her. I guess as long as the groomer allows me to stay with her, I'd be open to it."

"Taylor's Tails has a decent reputation. They're up on Main Street. Ask about special accommodations. I'd send you to Mickey's groomer, but he's not taking any new clients."

Must be nice to be in a position to turn away clients, Autumn thought. She did not want someone else to work on Chrissy anyway.

Back at the house, she Googled Taylor's Tails. The search showed Corinne Taylor as the proprietor. The name sounded familiar. She looked at the newspaper article and confirmed that she'd found Gary Martin. The website showed the hours for Taylor's Tails. She had a few more hours before they closed, so Autumn decided to stop by for an audience with Ms. Taylor.

In a flash, she realized she had forgotten to ask Steve about his pain medication and gave herself a mental reminder for the next time she saw him.

She loaded Chrissy into the car and assured her she would not be left at the groomer.

"Give me a signal if you don't like the person."

Chrissy panted and said *mroww* in agreement.

The slow ride from the house to the town center proved uneventful. Autumn's mind worked on the case and checked on Chrissy in the mirror. It distracted her from worrying about every car coming around the bend. She found a spot right out front of the white-washed brick building with a large square window and Taylor's Tails written above it in Comic Sans font, punctuated with paws of various sizes denoting dogs and cats.

A bell tinkled as they walked through the door. Dogs barked in the back of the shop. A window between the reception desk and service area allowed customers to view their pets being groomed. The smell of cheap dog shampoo permeated the air and the sound of high intensity blow dryers provided continuous background noise. Chrissy trembled.

Autumn lifted her from the floor and whispered "Don't worry. I'm not leaving you here." She put her back down.

The dull white walls with paint chipping here and there along the chair rail molding gave a worn look to the space. Pictures of various doggy cuts hung on the walls, along with a framed price list. A woman with long black hair greeted them. She wore thick black eyeliner that ended in an upward stroke that gave her a cat-like appearance. Wet spots covered her smock and clipped dog hair clung to the damp areas.

"Chrissy!"

Hmm, this must be Corinne.

She came around the counter and bent down to pet Chrissy. A sluggish wag ensued. It did not dampen Corinne's enthusiasm. Autumn expected a dog groomer to sense the mood of animals. Either she did not understand a dog's body language or chose to ignore it in front of the potential customer. She stood up and held out her hand. Autumn shook it, and her aversion to clammy hands like Corinne's rose up.

"I'm Corinne Taylor. I can't believe you brought me Chrissy!"

Chrissy moved arm's distance from Corinne and stretched.

"'I'm Autumn Clarke. I adopted her from the shelter."

"The shelter! I would have taken her myself if I thought she would end up in that awful place."

"I hear that a lot."

Seemed like everyone loved Chrissy, but no one had inquired about her after Martin's death. So many disingenuous people surrounded Gary and Chrissy.

"Gary used to bring her to get groomed. It was a sad day when I found him."

"What happened?"

"I went there like I always did with my little guys, Frick and Frack. We were supposed to go to the dog park. The door was open and he was lying on the floor. I touched his face and tried to shake him a little, but he was cold. Chrissy sat next to him, quiet, looking at me. And then she made a little mewling sound that broke my heart. Horrible."

"It must have been terrible for you. Quite a shock."

"You have no idea. We were good friends. Spent a lot of time together at the dog park, and so did our fur babies."

"So you called 911."

"Yes, and waited for them to arrive."

"And what about Chrissy?"

"The police contacted animal control and they took her."

"I guess they didn't let you have her," said Autumn. In her mind, she was thankful for the way it turned out.

Corinne hesitated. "Yeah. They said it's standard procedure or something."

Autumn suspected the authorities would rather have a pet in the hands of a caring individual rather than putting her in a crowded shelter. She let it go.

"What do you think was the cause of death?"

"My guess is a heart attack. He was stressed out between work and home. His girlfriends were fighting over him again. They made him crazy."

"Is it possible they might have had something to do with it?"

"Could be. They were jealous beyond belief. So, is Chrissy here to be groomed?"

Autumn was jerked out of detective mode by the sudden change in topic. Suspicion niggled at her mind, wondering why Corinne did not want to pursue the conversation about Gary. It was possible that she was just wanted to get back to work.

"Do you provide special services? I want to stay with her while she's groomed."

Corinne thought about it. Chrissy looked from Autumn to Corinne and back with worried eyes.

"Gary left her here, no problem."

"Since she's been through a lot, I'd rather not leave her. Can you do it while I wait?"

"Sorry. It would throw off our schedule."

"No problem. I've been doing okay grooming her at home, so I'll continue."

Chrissy's tail slammed against the floor in a flurry of relief. Autumn picked her up and received wet kisses on her cheek. Autumn kissed her ear. Corinne's eyebrows arched up and the corners of her mouth turned down.

"Looks like you two have become close."

"I love her to the moon and back."

"Seems like the feeling is mutual."

"Well, nice meeting you. If anything changes, I'll be in touch."

Corinne handed Autumn a business card and they returned to the car.

Chrissy stared at Autumn from her car seat. She made a low growling sound and Autumn became dizzy and nauseous. Her vision blurred and the world started spinning. She closed her eyes and found herself looking at long black hair hanging down over a woman's face. She viewed the woman out from under pure white bangs, bent over the body of Gary Martin. Her perspective shifted up and the person came into focus; a vision of Corinne stealing an expensive-looking watch from Gary's wrist and checking his pockets for anything else she could grab before she pulled out her cell phone to dial 911. No sign of Frick or Frack as Corinne had mentioned.

The vision began to fade, and Autumn noticed a peculiar twilight sensation when she reverted to her normal perception from Chrissy's. It still made her a little queasy. The discomfort lessened each time Chrissy sent her a vision, but still felt strange.

"Good friends, eh? I'm glad I don't have friends like her."

Autumn decided to mention the possibility of robbery to Ray. Despite of the truth, Chrissy would not make a credible witness. It would never hold up in court, let alone in Ray's eyes.

℔

Corinne wiped her sweaty palms as she watched Autumn and Chrissy leave her shop. The questions she was asking made her uncomfortable. There was no way she could know what happened after she found the body. Besides, she had pawned the Rolex.

When she left Chrissy, she thought the family might want her. Gary cared for that dog more than for Corinne. Sometimes it pissed her off. Her jaw clenched. He had no idea how Corinne felt about him. Gary was self-absorbed except when it came to Chrissy.

Autumn was stirring the pot, digging for something that was none of her business. A burglary charge would ruin her reputation in the community. Suspicion of murder would be worse.

℔

Autumn drove through the little town's main drag, passing a boutique, an antique shop, a second-hand bookstore, a few restaurants, and a gas station. She loved the quaint village where she grew up. Unexpectedly orphaned three months ago and her thirtieth birthday a couple of years away, the familiar surroundings brought her comfort. The close-knit community watched over her, with no need to explain what happened to her parents. They already knew.

She waved to Julie as she walked Teddy up the street away from Autumn's house. They were too far along to join them. Chrissy let out a high-pitched bark at Teddy to say hello. Teddy looked toward the car and barked at Chrissy.

Moments later, Autumn pulled into the driveway. She still missed seeing her father's silver Audi parked to the side of the doublewide driveway. She focused on seeing it in mint condition rather than the twisted mess it became afterward. The envisioning strategy came too late.

Her breathing became shallow and the hyperventilating began. Her body tingled and her face numbed. She could not remember what Dr. Wes told her to do. Far off in the distance a low growl and then a sharp bark tried to break through the panic. It repeated for minutes before it crystallized in her ears. Chrissy's insistence jarred her out of the panic attack. Her furry paws pounded on the edge of her car seat, unable to jump out and reach Autumn. She finally took a deep breath and remembered to feel her feet on the floor. Another breath and she reached over to assure Chrissy that everything was okay.

Chrissy glared at her as she removed her from the car seat, imparting her frustration at the inability to reach Autumn. She kissed Chrissy on the head and put her on the ground.

"I know. We'll move your car seat to the front."

Chrissy wagged her tail and grunted in agreement.

Out back into the warm afternoon air, Chrissy made a pit stop on the lawn while Autumn set out a bowl of water and a couple of snacks for Chrissy and an iced tea for herself. A wet-faced Chrissy jumped up to sit with her on the lounge chair. Autumn loved snuggling with her warm, soft body.

Laptop balanced on her legs, she searched the Internet for photos of Gary's girlfriends. Two women in tight outfits showing off their silicone upper-wares for the camera popped up with the names Alexis Davenport and Miranda Green. Imagining them fighting over Gary was easy, their deep-toned red nail salon claws ready to strike. She needed an introduction.

=17=

The accounting office of Brian Gottlieb was quiet except for the shuffling of papers. Light music floated through the space. His secretary greeted Ray with a welcoming smile.

"How can I help you?"

"I'm Detective Reed of the Knollwood police department. Is Mr. Gottlieb available?"

"Certainly. One moment."

She dialed Brian Gottlieb's extension and gained permission to bring the detective to his office. She waved for Ray to follow her down the hall and tapped on her boss's door.

"Come in," he said.

"Detective Reed to see you." She ushered him in and closed the door behind her.

Brian Gottlieb rose from his chair and piles of papers to extend his hand. Ray shook it.

"Please have a seat, Detective."

Ray sat. A diploma in accounting from NYU Stern and Gottlieb's framed CPA status decorated the left wall. Sports memorabilia occupied the credenza and windowsill.

"What can I do for you?" He gave Ray his full attention.

This visit was more pleasant than his experience with Vaughn Evans. As a seasoned officer, Ray had a keen sense of people, and this guy was as open as they come.

"I'm investigating the death of Gary Martin. I understand you are the accountant for Martin and Evans, LLC."

"That's correct."

"Vaughn Evans told me you found a discrepancy in the attorney trust account. Can you tell me more about that?"

"Vaughn called before you arrived and gave me permission to share the information."

Ray nodded his approval. At least Vaughn seemed to cooperate.

"An attorney trust account is where case settlements are deposited for client disbursement. This money is separate from the attorney's personal funds."

"Okay."

"I do a periodic audit of their attorney trust to ensure the integrity of the practice. Last month, things didn't add up."

"Can you be more specific?"

"In a nutshell, three hundred thousand dollars was missing."

"Is there a way to tell who took the money?"

"Four people have access to that account: Gary Martin, Vaughn Evans, Fran Barnes, and Lisa Coleman. They can all make deposits and withdrawals from that account. It's hard to pinpoint a specific person."

"Vaughn believes Gary stole the funds. What is your opinion?"

"Anyone with access to the account is suspect. There are a few common scenarios to consider when money goes missing. First is that the attorney borrows money from the trust account intending to pay it back. Second is using the money before the case is completed to pay expenses of the practice. Third is outright theft to pay for substance abuse, gambling problems, or some other reason. None of these is a legitimate use of the account, but I've seen it all."

"Was the practice struggling to pay bills?"

"No. Their checking account is healthy and has enough in it to cover expenses for the next few months at least."

"I understand that Gary lived a life of luxury. Would he need funds to support his lifestyle?"

"Gary made quite a bit of money. His personal finances were stretched, but unless he had something going on that I wasn't aware of, he should have been able to support himself."

"How about Vaughn? What is his situation?"

"His earnings are high, he pays his taxes, but I don't know much about his personal life. He plays it pretty close to the vest."

Ray had the same impression.

"What about the legal assistants?"

"I don't do their personal taxes. Lisa has only been with the practice for about a year and Fran is a Vaughn devotee, with him since he opened the practice."

Ray closed his notebook.

"Thank you, Mr. Gottlieb. You've been very helpful."

They shook hands.

"My pleasure, Detective. I'm at your service if you need anything for the case...or even for your own tax and financial solutions." He smiled.

Ray smiled back. If he ever needed an accountant, he would pick this one.

"I'll keep it in mind."

Ray left the office with a friendly wave from the secretary.

Ace beat his tail against the half-opened window when he saw Ray approach the vehicle. Ray jumped in and slammed the door. He gave Ace a good rub to his head.

"Hey, boy. Sorry it took so long."

Ace wagged his tail.

He clicked his seatbelt into place, and Autumn popped into his mind. She had been through a terrible experience and lost both parents in the process. Ray understood about trauma. His battle with post-traumatic stress disorder lasted years and eased when Ace came into his life. The tour as a Marine in Afghanistan left a mark on him, but with therapy, medication, and Ace, he channeled the pain into helping others first as a police officer and now as a detective.

Autumn exhibited symptoms of PTSD but would not discuss it. He recognized that place. PTSD makes strong people feel weak and reluctant to talk about it. He hoped Autumn would give him the chance to get close. Not just to help her through it, but because she was a sharp, attractive woman. The way she doted on Chrissy and her keen eye for detail added to her appeal. He could see them together for the long haul. First, she had to open up.

"Want to see Autumn and Chrissy soon?"

Ace banged his tail against the back seat. If Ray had a tail, it would wag along with Ace's.

Ray backed out of the parking space and headed to Corinne Taylor's dog grooming salon. He and Ace walked in, and Corinne recognized them.

"Detective! Is Ace here for a bath?"

Ace stood his ground.

"No, not today." Ace already had a groomer. Ray would not leave him with this woman anyway.

"Then how can I help you?"

Ray noticed how Corinne wiped her palms on her dirty apron and fidgeted in place.

"I have a few more questions about your discovery of Gary Martin's body."

Ray saw her swallow. "Okay." Corinne folded her arms across her chest.

"How long did it take after you saw the body before you called 911?"

"I don't know. Minutes, I guess."

"Did you do anything before that?"

She shook her head no and swallowed again.

"The family reported some things missing."

"Like what?"

"Did you notice anything out of place?"

"No, but I didn't really look around."

"Do you know anyone named Kitty?"

Corinne frowned. "Nope."

"Have you ever heard Gary talk about someone named Kitty?"

"Not that I recall. I probably would have remembered that since animals are my business."

"Okay, thank you Ms. Taylor. I may have more questions at a later time."

"At your service, Detective."

Ray left with the sense that Corinne was hiding something.

≈18≈

Anna Martin waltzed into the bank with papers authorizing her access to Gary's account. The woman at the window printed out the balance and handed it to her: $1,579.62.

"This can't be right."

The bank teller shrugged. "That's what's in the account, ma'am."

She could not even pay one month's mortgage for Gary's house with this. Anna already had the water turned off and the cell phone and cable services discontinued. *That realtor better hurry up and sell the house*, she thought. The bills Gary left behind were piling up and the mortgage on the house was due. With his debt, she would be lucky to come away with fifty thousand dollars.

Anna completed the paperwork transferring the account into her name, took out a couple of hundred dollars in cash, and stomped out of the bank, her hopes of a windfall in place of her annoying brother dashed. Maybe she could sell the car and get some money, if he did not owe a ton on that, too.

Outside she ran straight into Detective Reed.

"Hello, Ms. Martin."

"Detective."

"This is perfect timing."

"Not for me. It's been a rough day so far, and I'm really not in the mood to deal with you."

"Sorry to hear that, since it's not an option."

"What do you want now?"

"By any chance, did you just look at Gary's account information?"

"Yeah. So?"

"Care to share how much he has in there?"

"Not enough, that's for darn sure. Barely covers his bills that I now have to pay."

"Is this his only account?"

"As far as I know. If you find another one, let me know."

She started walking away.

"One more question."

She turned, trying to destroy him with a withering look.

"Did Gary have any nicknames for you?"

"I'm sure he had names for me but not anything endearing."

"Have you ever heard of someone named Kitty?"

"No, but I don't know his friends."

"Thank you, Ms. Martin."

She walked away without another word.

≈19≈

Autumn and Chrissy found a parking spot in front of Elegant Nails. The busy salon was in a converted townhouse on Acorn Lane, a side street off Main in downtown Knollwood. The powerful odor of acetone and nail polish overwhelmed the senses, and Chrissy sneezed and turned a glistening nose up to look at Autumn.

"We won't be long."

Chrissy's tail gave a surrender-flag wave.

Customers occupied every station with nail techs bent over the hands or feet of clients. Gray walls set off the black chairs and furnishings. Red shelving provided a pop of color to the bleak color scheme.

"May I help you?"

The girl behind the desk tried to hold a pen without ruining the wet hot pink polish on her extra-long sculpted nails. Short, spiked hair in lavender and pink topped off her creative style.

"I'm planning a bridal shower and want mani-pedis to be part of the festivities. Do you do private parties?"

"Sure, we can accommodate you. How many are in your party?"

"I'm thinking about five of us."

"No problem." She looked down at Chrissy. "The pooch, too?"

"Polished toe nails aren't Chrissy's style."

The receptionist shrugged. "You wouldn't see it anyway with all that fur covering her toes. It looks like she's wearing fuzzy bedroom slippers."

Chrissy wagged her tail at the girl, and she smiled.

"Yeah, we'll skip the puppy pedicure."

"Which date?"

"It depends. I'm trying to work around two regular customers of yours. Miranda Green and Alexis Davenport."

The woman sat back, stunned.

"I hope you're not bringing the two of them to the same event."

"Why not?" Autumn played ignorant.

"They had a fight in here. Something about the attorney who died. It was a scene! Hair pulling, cursing, threats." Her arms flailed as she described the battle.

The drama had brought excitement to an otherwise dull existence.

"What about him?"

"They found out they were both were dating him. Must have been some catch to start a fight like that."

"Sounds crazy! What kind of threats?" Autumn leaned in as though she was interested in local gossip.

"Alexis said she would kill Miranda and Gary both if they kept seeing each other."

"Wow, thanks for the heads up. Did you let the police know?"

"What for?"

"Well, he's dead and there was a threat against his life."

"She was just mad. I can't imagine Alexis actually doing anything."

Autumn nodded and decided to let Ray know. Besides, it gave her a reason to call him.

So when do they have appointments?"

"We're careful not to schedule them on the same day. Miranda comes in every other Tuesday and Alexis every other Thursday starting this week. Both at eleven. They always wanted the first appointment times. That's how they ran into each other."

"I'll talk to the bride about her preference for dates and get back to you."

The girl blew on her nails to hasten drying time.

"That's fine."

"C'mon, sweetheart."

Autumn tugged Chrissy to get moving before the girl asked her any questions. Outside the salon, they took deep breaths to clear their lungs of the toxic chemicals. Chrissy sneezed, clearing her sinuses. The thought of two adults battling in a public place shocked Autumn. She wondered how far a jealous rage would take them in private, especially Alexis Davenport.

She looked down at Chrissy. She knew how irresistible this furry munchkin was and decided to walk Chrissy outside the salon on the day of Alexis' next nail appointment. It would be easy to get Alexis to talk once she realized it was Chrissy. In the meantime, she wanted to check-in with Ray to tell him what she had learned and to invite Ace for a playdate.

⚡20⚡

Ray and Ace pulled their Jeep into the asphalt driveway of Autumn's house. Ace smelled the ground, let out a bark, and wagged his tail.

"Yep, this is Chrissy's house."

Chrissy's high-pitched bark on the other side of the door welcomed them. The door opened before they could knock.

"She's a great doorbell. Always lets me know who's here."

She stood aside, letting Ray and Ace into the foyer, admiring Ray's physique in his form-fitting gray T-shirt as he moved past her. Ray looked around. Chrissy and Ace rushed toward each other, nose-to-nose, with tails wagging like metronomes on full speed.

"Nice place."

"Thanks. My parents put a lot of work into it." Her voice cracked a little when she said the word *parents* but pulled back her emotions under Ray's observant gaze.

She turned and led them through the kitchen and out onto the patio. The table was set for lunch complete with a vase of seasonal flowers. Healthy snacks and water were nearby for Ace and Chrissy. The pair had found their way to the grassy area in the yard and frolicked together. Chrissy showed Ace the larger ball purchased for his visit. He pushed the ball with his nose before chomping down on it and taking a lap around the yard. Ray watched them playing and nodded his approval.

"I'm glad Ace is comfortable here," said Autumn, setting down bowls of guacamole and pita chips.

She filled their glasses with lemonade and invited Ray to sit. He seemed at home, an ease of posture and relaxed facial expression making Autumn happy she had invited them. This was a big step for her to reach out and connect with someone new. Since the accident, it had been hard for her to be with anyone other than people with whom she was already familiar. Ray was different. She did not have to explain. He was aware of what happened. He made her feel safe when he was not saying things that made her blush. Even then, she did not mind since the butterflies in her stomach were pleasantly distracting.

"Yeah. He doesn't take to most people. His work makes him an excellent judge of character."

He looked at Autumn and winked. She looked down and smiled at the compliment.

"So you went over to Vaughn's office?"

"You were right; weird energy from those people."

Autumn nodded, a mouth full of pita and guacamole preventing her from voicing her agreement. She chewed, swallowed, and took a sip of lemonade.

"What did you find out?"

"I'm not obliged to say, you know that."

"How about I guess? Something is up, because I saw Gary's house, and supporting a place that large would be hard to maintain from a financial perspective. Vaughn must know something."

"Vaughn said they fought about money."

"That's a common argument among business partners. I wonder if Vaughn is capable of murder. He's full of himself, but that's not a crime."

Ray chuckled. "That's for sure. I guess it's a good trait if he's your attorney, but not if you're trying to get information from him."

"I was thinking about Travis Mitchell, too. Drug dealer, threatened Gary's life. Someone with a criminal history would be more likely to act on his impulses."

"Playing psychologist?"

"I've researched articles about criminal behavior, and he seems to fit the profile."

"Could be."

"I was reading about the drug. Nasty stuff. It's the version made in illegal labs that is so deadly. He would likely have access to lab-created fentanyl."

"True. There've been reports of overdoses in the county, so it's available. And Travis was a big supplier."

Ray took a third scoop of guacamole and loaded it into his mouth. Chrissy barked and Ace let out one big bark in response. They were playing "try and catch me" taking turns teasing by pouncing low onto the ground in front of each other, then hopping side to side. Autumn and Ray laughed at their antics.

"The thing that concerns me most about the stories I read was the accidental exposure law enforcement has come across. One officer almost died."

"I heard about that." Ray brushed his hands of pita crumbs. A tiny bird landed on the patio and pecked at the bits of food.

"What precautions are you taking?" Autumn had not meant to sound like a mother worried about her child.

"Are you afraid something could happen to me?" Ray gave her that knowing smirk that drove her crazy.

"Yes…well, you're a nice person and…" She sipped her lemonade to hide her burning cheeks.

"I appreciate it. I wouldn't want anything to happen to you either." His smile shifted from smirk to caring.

Before her entire face turned beet red, she changed the subject, only half sorry she brought up her fear for his safety.

"Can you find out what Travis Mitchell has been up to?"

"I'll check it out if you promise to stay far away from looking into it on your own. This guy is dangerous."

She hesitated for a few beats. "Deal. How about some lunch?"

Ace and Chrissy trotted over to their snack station to gulp water and looked up smiling, faces dripping. Ray got up and ruffled the hair on Ace's head, then petted Chrissy. Autumn liked the way he interacted with his dog and with Chrissy. He was gentle and loving. A good sign.

&

After cleaning up from the visit, Autumn and Chrissy cozied up on the sofa and put on the television. Since the accident, Autumn had avoided the news because it tended to prompt anxiety. Now, with all that was happening in this case, it became a necessary evil. Her curious nature had reengaged, and the local broadcast gave her a sense of connection to the outside world. Besides, Chrissy's presence and her new relationship with Ray Reed, whatever it may turn out to be, strengthened her.

She kept the remote control in her hand with her finger on the channel button just in case she saw something that triggered her, like a car accident. She also changed the channel for anything that contained abused animals or starving children. Chrissy snored in her arms, tuckered out from her playdate with Ace. Autumn envied her ability to fall asleep at will.

A mugshot of a man with a thick neck and rough features filled the screen and a graphic identified him as Travis Mitchell. She raised the volume. The reporter stated that the body of Travis Mitchell was found in a field near the courthouse. He had made an appearance for a drug charge earlier that afternoon. His public defender plea-bargained his sentence down to community service. The toxicology report said he died of a fentanyl overdose.

Autumn sat up, waking Chrissy, who let out a little growl at being disturbed. She wondered if he treated himself to a hit of the drug to celebrate the court victory. There went her prime suspect in the death of Chrissy's pet parent. She dialed Ray to see if he heard the news. He picked up on the first ring.

"Did you hear about Travis Mitchell?"

"Yeah. He had just left the courthouse. He was arrested for drug-related offenses a week after he threatened Gary Martin and was out on bail."

"Would he have taken a chance of getting caught with drugs?"

"Hard to say. Some of these guys don't fear the law."

"Even so, I can't imagine him being so blatant as to bring them into the courthouse."

"You'd be surprised. Gotta run. How about lunch tomorrow at the café? 12:30?"

"Sounds perfect."

As she hit *end call,* she realized her heart was racing, but it was not a panic attack. It was excitement at seeing Ray again.

℞

Even after hearing Ray's soothing voice, the news of Travis' death shook Autumn. It made her feel uncomfortable, but she was not sure why. Walking helped her manage her anxiety and even though Chrissy was a reluctant participant, once she saw Mickey, she was more excited about the excursion. They were half a block into their walk when she asked Steve about his medication.

"I found out that Gary Martin died of a fentanyl overdose. My research showed that it's used in pain management. What did they give you to deal with your post-operative pain?"

"Physical therapy and a transdermal patch of fentanyl. Works wonders to get me moving, but it makes me a little wobbly so I only use it when I don't plan to leave the house."

"Sounds like strong stuff."

"Yes. It's a godsend. I got too used to the Oxy they had me on. It just didn't work anymore. The fentanyl helped me overcome the pain enough to get through PT."

Autumn and Steve saw Julie and Teddy up ahead. They waved, and Chrissy and Mickey pulled against their leashes trying to get to their friend, Teddy. The pet parents took a break while their charges sniffed and squatted.

"Another case of fentanyl poisoning came into the hospital today," said Julie shaking her head, her hair staying in perfect order. Autumn's hair required mousse and a tight ponytail to accomplish that feat.

"Another?" Steve said, concerned over the drug he was taking.

"First Gary Martin and now Travis Mitchell," Autumn replied.

"How did you know about the second one?" asked Julie, surprised how fast news travelled.

"On the news."

"Should I be concerned? I'm on it for pain," said Steve, raised eyebrows formed creases in his forehead.

"Not if it's legitimate from a pharmacy, you're opioid tolerant, and you're using it as prescribed," explained Julie. "There's lots of illegal fentanyl on the street. They mix it with heroin and other drugs. It's lethal. Two deaths in such a short period of time is cause for concern," said Julie.

"Opioid tolerant?" Autumn asked.

"Yes. If your doctor prescribes painkillers in the opioid class of drugs and the patient becomes resistant, then they prescribe fentanyl because it's much stronger. They still need to monitor the dosage."

Steve gulped. "I think I'll give my doctor a call."

"What happens if the patient isn't opioid tolerant?"

"Respiratory depression and death."

Autumn nodded, thinking about how this could play out in Gary Martin's case.

"Was there anything odd about the circumstances?" Autumn hoped to gain information that could point to Gary's killer.

"He was wearing a light jacket. A powdered form of the drug lined his pockets. He probably died within minutes."

"Just from touching the powder?" Steve asked, incredulous.

"Absorbed through the skin. The stuff is powerful and dangerous."

"I think I can tolerate the pain after all. I don't need this prescription."

"Don't go off it without consulting your physician. It's safer."

Steve nodded.

"But why would he bring drugs into the courthouse? He was there on a drug charge. He wouldn't want to get caught."

Julie shrugged. "There was no bag in his pocket. Just loose powder. Possibly residue from a previous delivery. I doubt anyone in the courthouse would notice."

"What about the fact that Travis Mitchell was found in a field?" Autumn asked.

"I know that area. There's a bus stop on the other side of the field from the courthouse. I bet he was taking a shortcut," Steve chimed in.

"And today's weather was a little cooler than expected, so he stuck his hands in his pockets to take away the chill," Autumn theorized, imagining Travis as he took his last walk through the field.

"Both Gary and Travis died of the same drug. They knew each other. Seems unlikely that both were accidental overdoses," surmised Julie.

"Agreed. They must be connected in some way," said Autumn.

Autumn's mind raced. If Travis had killed Gary and someone who cared for Gary found out about it, Travis Mitchell's death may be out of revenge. The list of women who cared about Gary numbered three that she knew of: Lisa Coleman, Alexis Davenport, and Miranda Green. Four, if she counted Gary's sister, Anna. Five, if Corinne Taylor wanted to retaliate against someone killing her friend, despite her loose definition of friendship. She decided to call Stephanie when she got back to the house.

છ

"Hey, Stephanie!"

"Autumn! It's been a while."

"Sorry I haven't been in touch. Things have gotten interesting around here."

"You're not sticking your nose into the Gary Martin death, are you?"

"Well..."

"Ugh. I thought we decided you were going to the police."

"I did. And it turned out better than I expected."

"Did they share information with you?"

"Not initially, but I've been working with the detective in charge of the case."

"What do you mean 'working'?"

Autumn smiled thinking of Ray and her stomach did an excited leap. "Well..."

"You already said that. I'm coming over there to get the scoop. I'll bring the wine."

Stephanie arrived as twilight set in over the quiet neighborhood. The lightning bugs flashed on the front lawn. Happy childhood memories twinkled in Autumn's mind. She and her friends had chased these magical insects and put them in ventilated jars, then let them out once playtime was over. Autumn was glad to see more of them now than in previous years. Their numbers had been waning due to lawn chemicals and other unnatural sprays people used to keep their gardens free of insects. Chrissy greeted Stephanie at the door, and a flurry of petting and wagging ensued.

Autumn opened the bottle of Chianti and poured a healthy serving into each glass. The water was boiling and she threw in the capellini and heated up the canned red clam sauce in the microwave. It was not her mother's clam sauce, but good in a pinch. Garlic bread was toasting in the oven.

Places were set in the dining room. Autumn sat with Stephanie to her right and Chrissy at her feet. Each woman took a forkful and sipped some wine.

"Mmm," Stephanie said, nodding her head in approval.

"Yeah, I've been in the mood for pasta since the night I met Lisa Coleman."

"Huh?"

"She's my neighbor's daughter. She was cooking pasta when I visited Steve's house. And she just so happens to be a legal assistant at Gary Martin's office."

Stephanie raised her eyebrow.

"What?" Autumn's attempt at playing innocent was not working.

"Don't you think it's dangerous to be prying?"

"I can call Ray if anything happens."

"Ray?"

Autumn smiled. Giddiness overtook her every time she thought of him. Saying his name set off a surge of sparkling energy through her body, forcing her shoulders up. Stephanie put her fork down.

"Boy, it's been an eventful ten days since I last saw you. No wonder I haven't heard from you."

Stephanie dabbed her mouth with a napkin and waited. Autumn looked at her plate, grinning with visions of Ray and Ace in her home. It was comfortable to have them here.

"He's the detective working on the Gary Martin case. I met him when I went to the police station. And then I ran into him in the dog park. He and his German shepherd, Ace, came over once.'"

Stephanie sat dumbfounded, eyeing Autumn with a knowing look.

"Your goofy expression reminds me of the beginnings of your brief relationship with Scott."

Autumn stopped mid-chew and then finished the mouthful with a gulp of wine. Stephanie's comparison tightened her stomach and made her wince.

"It's different from that. Ray isn't chasing me the way Scott did. And I trust him."

Stephanie took a bite of garlic bread, giving her time to digest this information.

"Okay. Say he's different. Let's assume that he has the best intentions. What's happened between you so far?"

"Nothing."

"Mmm hmm."

"No, really. We had lunch and he came over for a playdate with Ace and Chrissy."

Stephanie waited for more. Autumn took her time forking pasta into her mouth and chewing in a slow, deliberate manner. When Stephanie crossed her arms and tapped her foot, Autumn smiled and continued.

"He's kind of sweet, teasing me with suggestive comments, but never making a move on me. Drives me crazy."

Her friend nodded in understanding.

"Do you think you're ready for a relationship?"

"Before meeting him I didn't think I was. But having Chrissy around opened me to wanting one. Ray's dog and Chrissy get along great. It's still scary, though."

"Now you have two things to be careful of," Stephanie said, lifting her glass in salute to Autumn's realization.

"I'm going to take one day at a time. For right now, I'm puzzled by the death of Travis Mitchell and was hoping you'd help me figure it out."

"I'll try."

Autumn explained how they found him and the cause of death, finishing with the question *how did the fentanyl get into his pockets?*

"Well, you said he was a drug dealer. He might have had it on him and the bag broke."

"There was no bag in his pocket. And why would he bring it into the courtroom?"

"That's the problem. He wouldn't." Stephanie scrunched her lips together, puzzled.

They ate, and sipped wine in silence for a few minutes. The Chianti did not help trigger any answers to this dilemma.

"The only way would be for someone else to put it in his pockets," Autumn decided.

"But how did the fentanyl get into his pockets?"

"Someone who Travis Mitchell wouldn't suspect."

"Someone close to him with a reason to want him dead. Revenge. Maybe a business deal gone bad."

"Could be that the person hired a hit man to do it."

"Don't go all *TV-drama-series* on me. But the rest of it makes sense."

"Someone associated with Gary Martin's death? Or unrelated to that?"

Stephanie reached down to scratch Chrissy's silken ear. Chrissy looked up at her. "I think your baby needs a walk."

"How do you know that?"

"Odd, but it's like she's telling me what she wants."

Autumn smiled and got up to get Chrissy's harness.

Stephanie left after their walk, and Autumn and Chrissy curled up on the couch with a mystery novel. Chrissy snuggled between Autumn's leg and the sofa cushions. Autumn realized that she had forgotten to take her dose of anti-anxiety medication, but she was too comfortable to get up. She would tell Dr. Wes at Friday's appointment.

⸗21⸗

Autumn readied for her meeting with Ray. She took her morning meds to avoid an episode around him. In the back of her mind, the word *date* floated around, After all, he did ask her to meet him, but to presume would lead to disappointment. Staying in the moment was best, but the tingles in her stomach told her she wanted more.

She put on her slim jeans and her favorite pink T-shirt with a big daisy in the middle. Her reflection showed a confident woman, and the smile she wore was a nice accessory. She had not seen it in a long time. Chrissy's hair was fluffy and two pink bows held her pigtails.

The pair left early to stop at the nail salon hoping to run into Miranda Green, Gary's part-time lover. A parking spot awaited them on Main Street. Autumn loved window-shopping. She took her time while scanning the street for Miranda based on the photo she found online. Chrissy was the bait.

They walked past the side street that led to Elegant Nails, but the sidewalk was empty so they kept walking.

"She looks like a dog I know."

The woman's long blonde hair cascaded over a tight, red, V-neck top and white slacks. She looked down at Chrissy.

"Her name is Chrissy. I adopted her a couple of weeks ago. She belonged to an attorney named Gary Martin."

The woman's eyes widened, and she bent down to pet Chrissy's head. Chrissy wagged her tail.

"How are you doing you poor baby?" Then to Autumn, "I spent time with Gary."

"You did?" she said, trying to sound shocked. "I'm Autumn."

"Miranda. I wondered what happened to her after Gary passed."

"She went to the shelter. That's where I got her."

"I wish I had known. I would have taken her."

Chrissy moved closer to Autumn and sat leaning against her leg. Autumn reached down and scratched behind her ears.

"I hear that a lot. So how did you know Gary?"

"We dated. The bastard." She crossed her arms across her ample chest.

"Bastard?"

"Strung me along and cheated on me with that snake, Alexis. How could he fall for someone who parties as much as she does?"

"What if he had been partying, too?"

"Not like her. He was more of a drinker than a drug user. She liked to dabble in harder stuff. I'll bet she was high when she wrote the threatening emails."

"To Gary?"

"And to me! She said she wouldn't let anyone else have him. Who knows? She may have killed the poor jerk."

"You must have been scared."

"In a way. I decided to leave it alone, and I'd get back at him another way."

"How do you mean?"

"Slept with his partner, Vaughn."

Miranda's matter-of-fact tone and evil smile surprised Autumn. She did not relate to this type of behavior. Autumn blinked and petted Chrissy to detract from her shock.

"I'm sure that got him." She tried to match Miranda's nonchalant attitude.

"He was pissed. They were already fighting about something else, so that was the icing on the cake."

"What they were fighting over?"

"No clue. Don't care. I'm late for my nail appointment." She bent down and grabbed Chrissy under her chin a little too hard for Autumn's liking. "You take care." She trotted off down the sidewalk without a glance back at Autumn and disappeared into the nail salon.

It took Autumn a moment to gather her thoughts. Her hand hurt and realized that she had been clenching the leash, nails digging into her palm. Releasing it brought instant relief. She and Chrissy headed to the car, excited about sharing this information with Ray. She was glad that Miranda, or any of these other characters, had not adopted Chrissy.

&

Ray sat at what he considered their table, Ace relaxing underneath, until he saw Chrissy. He got up with such force that the table almost toppled. Ray and Autumn laughed at Ace, but they were just as excited to see each other. They admired one another, grinning.

Ray raised his hand in welcome, his heart quickening as she and Chrissy drew closer. The way the breeze blew Autumn's shiny hair made his stomach flutter. It was as though she stepped out of a shampoo commercial. Wow, he was really falling for her and felt awkward at these unfamiliar feelings. He reeled himself in, telling himself it was too soon to get involved. The bad relationships from the past left a sour taste in his mouth, yet Autumn seemed different from the others.

Chrissy and Ace ran toward each other, which inspired Ray to dispense with the hesitation and hugged Autumn in greeting. Relief washed over him as she hugged him back. He pulled out her chair, and she sat down, eyes sparkling. She grabbed his muscular forearm. Her touch sent warmth through his body.

"You're not going to believe what I just found out!"

A waiter came over and brought two lemonades and tuna sandwiches on multigrain bread. Autumn looked at the waiter and then at Ray.

"I remembered from last time. With mustard, right?" She nodded. He smiled and put his hand over hers. "Now what did you want to tell me?"

Ray's hand tingled where he touched her. Autumn stumbled over her words before she thanked him for lunch. Ray responded with a gleaming smile and a nod to continue. Autumn told him about her encounter with Miranda between bites of sandwich.

"Do you think Alexis could be a suspect?"

"I'm not ruling out anyone at this point. Especially those who had access to drugs."

"How about Miranda sleeping with Vaughn?"

"He accused Gary of embezzlement. It may have been his way of getting back at him."

Chrissy looked up from her bowl of water, commanding Autumn's attention. "You put up with a lot of difficult people, sweetheart." She petted Chrissy's head and, acknowledged, Chrissy nibbled at her crumbled hamburger patty.

Ray liked the way Autumn cared for Chrissy. He imagined what it would be like to be a regular part of her life as he sipped his drink.

"I can check into Alexis and question her. Please don't go back to the nail salon on her appointment day."

Autumn gave him a fake glare and laughed, unable to hold the look. "Okay, but promise you'll call me right after you talk to her."

"I promise." Ray intended to call her right after and beyond.

⸗22⸗

Miranda's uneasiness lasted through her nail appointment. It did not seem random to see Chrissy and her new owner. Autumn's interest in Vaughn and Gary was odd, coming from someone who did not know them. What did she know and what would that mean for Miranda herself?

She slid into the BMW, careful not to ding her nails as she fastened the seatbelt. Her emotions got the best of her during the conversation and probably revealed too much. Miranda dialed Vaughn's cell number.

"Hey, Miranda."

She knew Vaughn's moods, and he sounded tired.

"Everything okay?"

"I had another visit from Detective Reed."

"Great. What did he want?"

"He asked me about some things I shared with a woman who adopted Chrissy."

"Funny, I just ran into her myself."

"What did you tell her?"

"Probably too much. That Alexis threatened Gary and me and that I had revenge sex with you."

Vaughn groaned.

"She'll run back to her policeman buddy and tell him what you said."

"Why does she care, anyway?"

"Chrissy. If that dog wasn't involved, she wouldn't be snooping around."

"That's how she sucked me into a conversation. I recognized Chrissy."

"Don't do anything stupid. Just lie low."

"You don't give me enough credit."

The line went dead. Man, she really had a track record of picking losers.

≈23≈

Refreshed after seeing Autumn and Chrissy, Ray and Ace drove back to the station to research Alexis Davenport. He also searched the database for Dean Sanders. Anyone who threatened Gary or gave him unwanted attention was a suspect. Now there was also Travis Mitchell's death.

No bag in the pockets, according to the medical examiner, and with pockets lined with fentanyl, it seemed planted. Travis was a seasoned drug dealer. He knew how to avoid accidental poisoning. Who would want Travis Mitchell dead? Were the deaths of Gary Martin and Travis Mitchell connected? And if so, there must be an individual who had a motive to kill them both.

Ray scrolled through the police database to learn more about Dean Sanders. The screen flashed and brought up arrests for running an illegal gambling business. He must have had a slick lawyer to get him off the charges. So why would he be chasing down Gary Martin?

As far as Autumn's information about threats made by Alexis Davenport, he would need proof. He scrolled through Gary's text messages and found a few from Alexis, threatening both Gary and Miranda, telling them they would be sorry and that they did not want to test her. Hate spewed from the words and he finally found what he was looking for: Alexis outright saying that she wanted to kill them both. Did Gary sent his last text to her, saying they could work something out? What would connect Alexis to Travis, unless he was her drug source?

Ray was grateful for Gary Martin's cell phone and for the information Autumn provided him. And of course for Chrissy getting a loving new home that brought him the woman with whom he saw himself spending the rest of his life.

Ray noted down Dean Sanders' and Alexis Davenport's addresses and led Ace out to their vehicle.

∞

Dean Sanders lived in the historical section of Knollwood. This area contained the original homes built one hundred fifty years ago. The sycamore, cedar, and maple trees soared above the power lines and sometimes fell over in storms, cutting off electric service to the area.

Ray drove his unmarked SUV at a crawl, straining to see the house numbers that were not always present. He would recommend that the fire chief do a complete inspection. Houses with no street number are harder to find, which delays response time in case of an emergency.

He found Dean Sanders' worn blue clapboard house by deducing his address from his clearly marked neighbors. A dull gray 1990s Toyota Camry sat in the driveway, and dingy curtains covered dirty windows. Ray parked the car out front and left Ace behind. His hard knock carried authority. A minute passed. His hand raised to knock again when the door creaked open and a disheveled man peeked around the edge.

"Dean Sanders?" said Ray.

"Yes?" His voice creaked through a few days' worth of facial hair.

"Detective Raymond Reed of the Knollwood Police Department. May I have a few moments of your time?"

Ray showed him his badge.

Dean hesitated and then opened the door the rest of the way. He cowered behind it as Ray entered, glanced up and down the street, and then closed the door. He led Ray into the living room just off the entry hall. Sanders pointed to a worn upholstered chair frayed at the edges and sat himself on the sofa. Dean's eyes darted around the room. He waited for the detective to start the conversation.

"You seem a bit jumpy Mr. Sanders."

He nodded.

"Want to tell me about it?"

Ray kept his body relaxed and arms open to make Dean Sanders comfortable.

He looked at the ground. "What if I'm next?"

"Next for what?"

"To die!" He clutched himself and rocked.

"What makes you think that would happen?"

"First Gary Martin, and then Travis Mitchell. I'm probably next."

"How are you connected to those two men?"

"I never should have listened to Vaughn."

"Vaughn?"

"Evans! Told me to contact his partner, saying he had the money. Said to use the code words 'legal representation' to talk about the money so we wouldn't get caught." Dean Sanders shook his head in disbelief.

"How much money are we talking about Mr. Sanders?"

"Three hundred thousand dollars."

Ray sat with this revelation for a moment, letting it sink in. Vaughn owed money? After he talked about Gary being the one in debt? The embezzled amount was around three hundred thousand dollars, the same as he owed Dean Sanders. No wonder it seemed that this guy was stalking

Gary to represent him. It also put Gary squarely in the middle of the embezzlement allegation.

"Who are you afraid of Mr. Sanders?"

"I owe my broker big time. Plus, Vaughn Evans is out to protect his own hide. I don't trust him."

"What makes you nervous about the deaths of Gary Martin and Travis Mitchell?"

"They were murdered! It had to be Vaughn. He was always bad-mouthing Gary about his partying. He might have used Travis to supply drugs for a convenient overdose."

"And what about Mr. Mitchell's death?"

"Vaughn is a sharp cookie. He would have saved some of the stuff to use on Travis. I listen to the news. I know it was fentanyl poisoning. That was Travis' specialty."

"So you think you're next because the other two are dead?"

"Sure. I'm the only other person who knows about this mess." His arms wrapped tighter around himself.

"Are you able to provide a sworn statement to this effect, Mr. Sanders?"

"Why would I do that?"

"Because it's better than being taken down to the station for illegal gambling. With your prior history, you may be facing jail time. A judge might be more lenient if you give me the evidence I need."

Dean chewed his lower lip. "That would make me a snitch. If word got out, I'd be through in the bookie business."

"We can do it right here, Mr. Sanders. No one will know. I'll keep it in the file until it's needed. Afterward, I suggest you go stay with a friend or relative."

Sanders nodded, his mouth down turned and eyes averted. He got out a pen and started writing. Ray made sure all the details were included and the signature at the end secured it under penalty of perjury.

&

With Detective Reed out the door, Dean ran upstairs to pack. He decided not to make any calls to alert anyone who might be listening of his travel plans. As Gary Martin's stalker, he might become a suspect in his murder. The confession he signed with the detective somewhat allayed his fears, but he did not trust the legal process, especially since Vaughn could turn the tables on him at any moment.

Vaughn Evans proved to be underhanded and manipulative. He could create any scenario he wanted with a well-placed legal argument that would land squarely on Dean's head. He wondered if Vaughn had killed Gary or if he had someone else do it. Who knew where other players had lain in wait to serve Vaughn's purpose? The worst-case scenario was circumventing the court system and false justice served by one of his cronies.

His own broker scared him, as well. It might be possible to send him over to collect from Vaughn directly. Dean's plan was to disappear and not worry about this mess. He limited the packing to one suitcase, locked the door behind him, and said goodbye to his house as he drove away.

≈24≈

Autumn's heart gave a little flutter when she heard Ray's voice on the phone. He told her he met with Dean Sanders and that it was a good lead but he could not share the information just yet. No amount of begging could get him to do anything but chuckle at her attempts to get it out of him. It did get her what she hoped was a date for later today, and a vow to tell her when he could. Ray also released her from her promise not to talk to Alexis, since the new information relaxed his concern that Autumn might be interviewing a murderer.

She was glad that she did not have to go against her word to Ray. That was no way to start a relationship and she wanted this one built on a solid foundation, unlike her others. Trust was a key component. It was essential for her to display the trustworthy behaviors she wanted from Ray.

So here she was on Main Street, wanting to satisfy the gnawing feeling that Alexis was somehow involved in this case despite Ray's sense that she was wasting her time. At the least, she would get a better sense of Gary Martin, and Chrissy might provide some additional information after the meeting. She hoped that Alexis Davenport would spot Chrissy on her way to the nail salon the way Miranda had.

The window-shopping ploy worked once again. Shop owners came out to say hello to Chrissy and brought her bowls of water or a snack. She was popular on Main Street. Autumn was glad that Chrissy made them feel happy with her sweet disposition and wagging tail. With her grain-free diet, her skin and hair were soft and smooth. She rarely scratched, but Autumn did not want to make people feel bad about the snacks they offered. An occasional treat that was off her diet was fine, just like Autumn going off of her own healthy eating when she craved red licorice candy. Everything is best in moderation. Most of the time, Chrissy took the snack and spat it out where no one could see her. Autumn wished she had that kind of self-control.

Chrissy's tail waved in recognition at a woman parading toward them in high heels and form-fitting slacks. Her filmy blouse billowed with her movement. She flipped her long, blonde hair and adjusted her designer sunglasses before realizing who she was looking at.

"Chrissy!"

Autumn smiled. Chrissy was the best bait she could ask for.

"Hello," she said to the stranger, who she guessed was Alexis.

"Hi." She continued to pet Chrissy, happy to see her.

"How do you know Chrissy?" Autumn fished.

"She was my boyfriend's dog. How did you get her?" the woman said in an accusing tone.

"Adopted her from the shelter."

"Shelter! You poor baby." The petting became more pronounced than before.

Not taking the hint, Autumn became more direct. "I'm Autumn Clarke. And you are?"

She looked up from her crouch, "Alexis Davenport."

"So you're one of Gary Martin's girlfriends."

"His involvement with Miranda was over." She glared at Autumn. "I was his only girlfriend. What's it to you anyway?"

"Chrissy is important to me. I want to know about the people who raised her."

Alexis pet Chrissy one more time before raising to eye level with Autumn. She crossed her arms.

"She was raised just fine."

"I'm not saying she wasn't. It's just that she has separation anxiety and having stayed with Gary's body overnight either triggered it or made it worse."

Alexis lowered her gaze and adjusted the shoulder strap of her purse. She swallowed. "I heard about that. It must have been terrible for her," she mumbled.

It was Autumn's turn to cross her arms. "Was it a shock to hear about Gary?"

Alexis looked away. "Yes, it was."

"Chrissy seems happy to see you."

"Gary brought her when we met for drinks earlier on the evening he died. We were at an outdoor patio that allows dogs."

"Where was that? I'm trying to find more places to take her."

Alexis hesitated. "Knollwood Inn."

"Good food?"

"Yeah, I guess."

"Sad that you didn't know it would be the last time you'd get to see him. Did he seem ill?"

"No, he seemed okay. Listen, I need to get to my appointment. Chrissy, you be a good girl." Alexis petted her one last time and walked away without another word.

Autumn noted the discomfort and the lack of sadness at remembering the last time Alexis saw Gary. It was puzzling. She knew how heart wrenching the memory is when you don't realize it is the last time you will get to see someone. A pang of melancholy filled her chest. She shoved it down, felt her feet on the sidewalk, and refocused on Chrissy. The little face upturned, keeping an eye on her mommy. Autumn, overcome with love, scooped her up, and held her close. She kissed her ear and walked back to the car.

With Chrissy tucked into her car seat, Autumn phoned Ray and asked him to meet her at Knollwood Inn.

&

Autumn and Chrissy got there first and waited in the parking lot, enjoying the lavender-scented breeze that drifted through the open windows. The Knollwood Inn was all brick, surrounded by English gardens loaded with lavender, among other June-blooming perennials. Flagstone patios tucked here and there added to the ambience. The cozy dining area was inviting, surrounded by an ornamental black wrought iron fence.

Ray pulled up next to them, Ace sitting in the front seat, strapped in with a special seat belt designed for large dogs. They looked over and smiled, Ace's smile wetter than Ray's. They got out of their cars and Autumn admired Ray, still dressed in a suit from work. He hugged her and then helped Chrissy out of her car seat, giving her a hug as well. Chrissy licked his cheek, and he chuckled. Watching them lifted Autumn's heart.

They approached the outdoor dining host, who glared at the two dogs.

"Good evening. I'm sorry, but there are no dogs allowed."

Ray looked at Autumn, brows furrowed.

"Are there times when you do allow dogs?" Autumn asked, suspicious of Alexis' story.

"Only service dogs are permitted."

"Good thing Chrissy is a service dog, then. And Ace is a police dog."

The host's eyebrows went up. Autumn pulled out Chrissy's official documents and showed them to her. Ray flashed his badge. The host handed back the papers, nodded, and opened the gate to the outdoor patio.

"Welcome to the Knollwood Inn."

Longer hours of sunlight made evening outings more fun and pushed away dark thoughts from Autumn's mind. Autumn put her arm through Ray's as they followed the host down the flagstone path to the patio. He squeezed her arm in the crook of his. Autumn was startled. She had not realized what she did until he made her aware of it. It happened so naturally and Ray did not seem to mind, so she stayed connected to him. The host led them to a table in the shade.

Ray pulled out her chair and she sat, Chrissy at her feet. Ace sat upright next to Ray.

"I thought you said they allow dogs here."

"That's what Alexis Davenport told me. She said she and Gary Martin had drinks here the night he died."

"Was Chrissy a registered service dog then?"

"No."

Autumn gulped a breath, realizing that she had let her secret out. Ray waited for an explanation

"Chrissy is an ESA, emotional support animal. I have her because I developed PTSD after the accident." She squinted at the potential reaction to this news.

Ray nodded. "I get it. That was one of the worst crashes I've ever seen. Losing both your parents in an instant is traumatic. You barely made it out alive."

Autumn looked down. She felt Ray's finger gentle under her chin, encouraging her to look at him. Her eyes filled with tears.

"I'm sorry I didn't tell you before."

"Don't worry about it. I've got a little PTSD myself from some of the professional situations I've been in and from my military experience."

"So you don't think I'm crazy?" Autumn was relieved to have it out in the open. Chrissy could now wear the pink ESA vest she received in the mail.

He looked at her sideways and lifted the right side of his mouth. The look made her laugh and released a tear from the corner of her eye. Ray wiped it away and held her hand across the table. She looked up at him, eyes glistening. He brought her hand to his lips and kissed her fingers.

"Now, let's figure out what to eat and you can tell me everything Alexis said."

"Deal." She dabbed at her eyes and then nose with a tissue retrieved from her purse.

The menu was limited but had offerings of meat, fish, poultry, and vegetarian options. She ordered crab cakes and he got the steak, knowing he would have to share with Ace. They opted for iced teas, not wanting to drink and drive. Chrissy's bowls for water and special food were set-up off to the side of the table. Autumn even brought a water bowl for Ace, which he lapped up with delight.

Ray grabbed her hand again. Autumn liked the feel of it and was happy that their relationship seemed to be moving forward. She told him about her encounter with Alexis. He listened without interrupting. He let go of her hand when the salads came.

"She seemed guilty of something. Couldn't look me in the eye and was eager to get away from the conversation."

"Well, obviously she couldn't have come here that night, so we know she's lying about something."

"I didn't want to push."

"Smart girl. I'll contact her and see what I can find out."

The entrees arrived, and the server said that Chrissy and Ace impressed her; they were so well behaved that she did not realize they were lounging under the table. Autumn and Ray smiled at the compliment and each petted their good dog.

"Let's eat and talk about something else," Ray suggested, picking up his knife and fork. He tried the garlic-mashed potatoes.

"Like what?"

"Like us."

Autumn stopped mid-chew and looked at Ray. Washing down the food with some tea, she gave a closed-mouth smile in case there was lettuce in her teeth. *Can this really be happening?*

Feeling a coy response was best, she replied, "What about us?"

"I know you feel it, too."

Autumn felt Chrissy's soft hair sweep against her leg. She looked down to see Chrissy looking up at her, smiling, encouraging her to open up.

"Like the fact that you seem trustworthy?" Autumn grinned.

"Chrissy likes me. Isn't that the best endorsement you could have?"

Autumn looked down and Chrissy smiled and wagged her tail.

"That's true."

"And Ace likes you, so he gave me the green light to bring this up."

Autumn wiped her mouth and put the cloth napkin in her lap. The scent of calming lavender wafted across their table.

"It's scary, though. Everyone I've ever loved is gone."

"I get it. You think I've never been hurt?"

Autumn waited a beat. "Can we take it slow?"

Ray smiled and took her hand.

"You're worth the wait."

≈25≈

Alexis clenched her jaw throughout her nail appointment. Autumn had taken her off guard. Under that sweet exterior was a probing intellect waiting to catch Alexis in a lie. She had not met Gary for lunch the day of his death. They had planned to go to the Knollwood Inn at some point, but Gary was reluctant since he could not bring Chrissy.

That fur ball had sucked her in. Admittedly, it looked like Autumn was taking good care of her. Seeing Chrissy made her miss Gary. Since his death, she had created a fantasy world about their relationship. The vision was strong enough that it went against the reality of his death and their actual relationship.

Her threats against Gary and Miranda did not help the situation. It made him wary of her, and he pulled back. In the aftermath of her rant, she regretted going after them, especially since the emails were a permanent record of her deadly threats.

She slammed her hand against the steering wheel. A dull ache started. Had she made a bad situation worse by lying to Autumn? How would she know the difference anyway? Besides, she was not a cop, so it should not matter.

Alexis pulled up to the Sunset Tavern, not remembering the drive over, just like on the day Gary died.

ϨϽ

Chrissy and Autumn sat in the car and waved goodbye to Ace and Ray. Her heart filled with joy at Ray's desire to be with her. As Autumn fumbled with the car keys, a wave of nausea overtook her. Chrissy stared at her from the passenger seat.

A vision of Alexis appeared. She looked like a giant frothing at the mouth. Her face scrunched in anger, her finger jabbing at the air in front of Gary. Chrissy's fear was palpable. Gary took a step back holding his hands in front of him before the vision faded.

Autumn shook off the shift in perspective and met Chrissy's eyes.

"That must have been scary for you and your daddy." She stroked Chrissy's soft head to calm them both.

Alexis had a temper, that was for sure. Who knew what she was capable of during an outburst?

Ray read the Gary Martin case file. This was the fifth time that week. His gut told him he was missing something.

He flipped through Gary's cell phone. Gary's text with Kitty was still odd. Anna Martin wanted Gary's nonexistent money but had a verifiable alibi of being with her parents the night Gary died, but that did not mean she had not hired an accomplice. Travis Mitchell was dead, so even if he had helped Anna Martin, he could not question him and there was no direct evidence of their partnership. Vaughn Evans had a financial motive, as well, and no real alibi. Corinne Taylor's statement sat staring at him in the open file folder. Maybe there was a connection.

He looked up the address for Taylor's Tails, grabbed Ace, and drove over to Corinne's grooming shop. Ace hesitated to enter, and Ray sensed his worry that he was in for a grooming.

"It's okay, buddy. Not today."

Ace's stance relaxed and he moved forward into the shop. The noise of dryers and barking made his ears twitch. Ray patted his head.

Corinne blew the dark, stringy hair out of her eyes and called to them from across the shop. "Back so soon?"

Ray wondered if she ever washed her work apron or her hair for that matter.

"I have a few more questions. May we speak privately?"

The office suited her with papers strewn across the desk, floor coated in grime, and a dog calendar on the wall. She pointed to a wooden chair covered in dog hair.

"I'll stand."

Corinne shrugged, sat behind her desk, and crossed her arms.

"In your statement you indicated that Gary Martin was dead when you found him. How did you determine that?"

"He wasn't moving." A brief smirk flashed across her mouth.

"He might have been unconscious."

"I didn't see him breathing."

"Did you touch the body?"

"No."

"Did you notice anything unusual?"

"Chrissy was next to him, shaking."

"And what did you do?"

"I tried to pick her up, but she growled at me and crouched down so I couldn't get a hold of her."

Ray pictured Chrissy upset about Gary and having to deal with this snippy woman on top of it. He was glad that she was in Autumn's capable hands.

"What happened when the police arrived?" Ray arrived at the scene after Corinne gave her statement.

"I told them the story that's in the report."

"Did you have a predetermined time to meet to go to the park?"

"No. I would stop by on the weekends to see if Gary and Chrissy wanted to join me and my dogs."

"How did you get in?"

"The door was wide open."

"The family reported several things missing from the house."

Corinne gulped. "So?"

"Do you know anything about the missing items?"

Corinne hesitated, her folded arms squeezed tighter.

"How would I know?"

Ray nodded and made a note. In his peripheral vision, he saw Corinne crane her neck to see what he was writing.

"Did you notice if Mr. Martin was wearing a watch?"

Her lips pressed together. "His sleeve was over his wrist, so I don't know. He may have been."

Ray made a note to review the photos of the crime scene to see if that were true.

"That's all for now, Ms. Taylor. I'll be in touch if there's anything else."

She squinted as though hit with a sudden punch. Ray turned to leave, noticing that Corinne Taylor stayed seated, looking like a wrung-out rag doll.

≈27≈

Settled in Dr. Wes' office, Autumn told him about forgetting to take her medication.

"What made you forget to take it?"

"I was distracted working on who murdered Chrissy's daddy."

"How did you feel?"

"Fine. I didn't have an episode, but took my evening dose."

"Are you considering reducing your dose?"

"I'm not sure."

"Let me know when you haven't had a panic attack for at least a week and we can talk about lowering your dose. We need to take you off of it gradually, so make sure you take your medication as prescribed for now."

"I will."

"What's this about investigating a murder?"

"You know about Gary Martin, Chrissy's former pet parent. It wasn't a heart attack. I want Chrissy to have closure, so I'm talking to suspects."

"Chrissy needs closure?"

"It's hard to explain. I can sense her distress over what happened to her daddy."

Dr. Wes scribbled in his notebook.

"What about the danger involved?"

"I'm working with a Knollwood Police Department detective, so he's keeping an eye on me." Autumn's eyes twinkled at the thought of Ray.

Dr. Wes nodded. He put a pen to his lips.

"Tell me more about him."

Autumn broke into a wide grin.

"His name is Ray and we've become close to him and his dog, Ace."

"What do you mean by 'close'?"

Autumn couldn't stop smiling and it transferred to Dr. Wes.

"We really like each other and decided to have a relationship." She hesitated. "I told him we need to take it slow."

"What was his reaction to taking it slow?"

"He was fine with it. I accidentally revealed that Chrissy is an ESA. He understands completely about my PTSD, since he knows the severity of the accident. As a bonus, he worked through his own post-traumatic stress from work and military service."

"It must be a relief to have someone in your life who understands what you're going through."

"Yes! And it gives me hope, too. Ray is well-adjusted, and if he can move through his trauma, so can I."

"Opening yourself to Ray means you're making a lot of progress. At the same time, there seems to be a bit of reluctance around it, even though you sound happy."

"I can't stop thinking about my parents' death. I've lost the people I love most in the world. What if I lose Ray, too?"

Autumn swallowed. It was hard to talk about them without her emotions getting the best of her. A tear slid down her cheek. She grabbed a tissue. Maybe it was too soon to get off her meds.

"You've had a severe trauma in losing your parents. The reaction to this type of emotional wound is different for everyone."

Autumn nodded. "I guess."

"You have someone who cares enough to honor your request for a gradual relationship to build. He shares your experience, recognizes the severity of the accident, and is willing to provide support."

Autumn picked up Chrissy, hugged and kissed her and settled her on her lap as she considered his words.

"Remember how reluctant you were about getting a dog? Maybe even more hesitant than having a man in your life."

Autumn chuckled. Dr. Wes's words rang true.

"Ray sounds like he's good for your emotional wellbeing. His presence is valuable and could speed up the healing process."

"He is a positive presence. I feel good when he's around. Safe...and a little giddy."

"You've learned through your relationship with Chrissy that having a loving bond is a mood elevator. Especially when you trust that person or pet." He smiled. "It can even make you forget to take your meds."

Chrissy looked up and smiled at each of them in turn. Autumn kissed her ear. Dr. Wes shook his head.

"She is really amazing. I've never seen an animal emote like she does."

"Chrissy likes him. Too bad I didn't have her to warn me about Scott." She gave a wan smile.

Chrissy gave one bark in agreement.

"She may be a good indicator, but it's important that you also trust your instincts when it comes to relationships."

"How do I do that?"

"See how your body tenses or relaxes when the person is around. You can use this on Ray or anyone who comes around you."

"I can see that. In speaking to some of Gary Martin's acquaintances, most of them made me tense or feel heavy."

"Exactly. Stay mindful of that type of involuntary reaction and trust it."

"Have you ever been afraid to love, Dr. Wes?"

"Everyone has been afraid of getting hurt at one time or another."

"It's more than that." Autumn took a breath. "What if I give my heart to Ray and he's taken away?'

"That's the scariest thing that could happen, isn't it?'

"Yes."

"Your parents were taken, and it's been a rough road. You opened your heart to this precious little girl knowing that your time together is limited."

"True."

"One day, nature will take her."

"The thought makes me sad, but I love her so much. Our time together makes me want to take a chance at loving and being loved."

"There's always a chance of losing those we love, but it doesn't mean we should avoid the experience of giving and receiving love. And Ray is in a high-risk profession."

A tear dripped down her cheek. She shook her head. "I'm afraid."

"You can always close yourself off, stay in the house, and decide that getting hurt is too upsetting to take the chance."

Autumn looked up, her eyes wide at the thought. She pictured herself alone in her living room, the years passing with no one to share her life.

Dr. Wes continued. "Or, you can allow love into your heart, the way you've done with Chrissy, and make the most of every moment."

Sighing, Autumn nodded. "That feels better than becoming a hermit." She offered a weak laugh.

"And you grew up in a loving household. Your parents gave you a foundation of love. You know how it feels to grieve because you know what it is to love."

"They did teach me how to love with my whole heart. It feels empty not giving my love to someone. Chrissy brought love back into my life. She is showing me how to have hope again. Even though I know I'll lose her one day, I'm not afraid to love her."

Dr. Wes nodded.

"I think loving her brought Ray into my life."

"How so?"

"Chrissy opened my heart, and Ray felt the love I have to give. After Scott, I thought I'd never find someone I could trust. But Ray is protective and makes me feel like everything is going to be okay. He and his dog came over, and we had a wonderful time. It feels right. It's easy to be with him. Chrissy loves his dog, Ace, and has taken to Ray."

"Dogs have good instincts when it comes to the quality of people."

"I trust her. She trusts me."

"Think how hard it must be for her to do that. She lost someone dear to her. She suffers from separation anxiety just as you do. Yet both of you have opened your hearts to one another."

Autumn smiled and brushed her fingers against Chrissy, who snuggled against her hand.

"My mother used to say that love is the greatest healer."

Dr. Wes nodded his agreement. "Your mother was a wise woman."

⸗28⸗

Ray's last stop of the day was the Sunset Tavern. He acquired Alexis Davenport's address from her driving record. The photos in Gary Martin's phone showed him what Alexis looked like beyond her deer-in-the-headlights driver photo. More research uncovered her employment as a bartender at the Sunset Tavern.

It was dim inside the tavern despite the bright afternoon. He was glad the law prohibited smoking in bars, so his suit would not absorb the noxious odor of cigarettes. There were about ten people scattered in pairs throughout the booth area, eating lunch. The red vinyl of the booth benches extended to the bar seats, where a few patrons drank alone.

He spotted Alexis behind the bar, wiping the counter. The black, short-sleeved bar uniform top was unbuttoned to the fourth button to reveal maximum cleavage for maximum tips. Her wavy blonde hair reached down her back and over her shoulders. She gave him a broad smile as he sauntered up to the bar and took a seat. He smiled back as he flipped his badge and then tucked it inside his suit pocket. Alexis' smile faltered and turned into a grimace.

"How can I help you, officer?"

"Detective Reed. Wanted to ask you some questions about Gary Martin."

She rubbed her neck and straightened her collar, her eyes averted from his steady gaze.

"What about him?"

"I understand you two were in a relationship and that you threatened the deceased and Miranda Green by email."

"What happened to privacy?"

"Nothing is private in the digital world. When was the last time you saw him?"

"The day he died. We met for drinks at the Knollwood Inn."

Ray wrote in his notebook that it was the same story she had told Autumn.

"I understand he took his dog everywhere with him. Was she with you at the Inn?"

"Yeah, he loved that dog more than he loved me." Her distaste was palpable.

"The Knollwood Inn doesn't allow dogs, Ms. Davenport."

Her eyes glazed over and her throat caught.

"Uh…"

Ray let her flounder for a few beats then softened his voice.

"Now, can you tell me where you last saw Gary Martin?"

Her eyes lowered and she sighed. Ray could tell she was debating what to tell him. He had seen it many times when interrogating a suspect. He opened his posture to invite her to tell the truth.

"Well, uh, maybe I should have my lawyer present."

"What are you afraid of?"

She pressed her lips together and looked him up and down.

"I'll tell you what I know if you promise to leave me alone after that."

"You've threatened two people, Ms. Davenport. I'll take your statement into consideration, but can't promise you anything."

She stared at him, deciding whether to trust him.

"We had a fight on the phone that afternoon. I told him Miranda slept with his partner, Vaughn, and he didn't believe me. I tried to convince him it should just be him and me but he was mad about what I said about Miranda."

"How did you know they slept together?"

"Vaughn is as conceited as it gets. I heard him bragging about it on the phone when I went to see Gary at the office one day. Gary's door was closed, so he didn't hear it."

"Did anyone else hear the conversation?"

"Not that I know of. The secretaries weren't at their desks. I was there to go to lunch with Gary…and Chrissy, of course."

Ray made a note. Another strike against Vaughn.

"So then what happened?"

"I felt sorry about the fight and went to his house to make up."

Her voice croaked. She filled a glass with water and took a gulp. Ray waited.

"The door was wide open and Gary was on the floor just inside with Chrissy sitting next to him. He wasn't moving, and I didn't want to touch him in case he was dead."

Ray frowned. "Why not?"

"Prints! I didn't want to leave any."

She was more self-absorbed than he thought.

"What did you do then?"

"I left. It sucked leaving Chrissy sitting there, but I didn't want any part of it."

"Any part of what?"

"Gary's death. My name in the news."

"How did you know he was dead? Did you try calling 911?"

"He wasn't moving. It didn't look like he was breathing either. Chrissy was crying."

It was the same story as Corinne's report of the scene. This was not the behavior of a woman in love. She did not even call 911 to report his condition. Ray's personal definition of love was selfless. He could not imagine Autumn doing something like that.

"Where did you go afterward?"

"I drove home and had a drink. I was shook up."

"Did Gary have any pet names for you?"

"Sometimes he called me 'babe' or 'hon,' why?"

"Do you know any named Kitty?"

"No."

"Okay, Ms. Davenport. Thank you for speaking with me. If there is anything else, what's the best number to reach you?"

"So I'm not in trouble?"

"That's all for now."

⣾

Chrissy and Autumn arrived home and ate lunch. Chrissy had some grain free beef jerky and Autumn had a salad with avocado and almonds. The session with Dr. Wes had been intense, so a nap was in order. Crying always made her feel tired. She opened the back door and Chrissy scampered out to the lawn and then back to the lounge chair where Autumn stretched out. She lifted Chrissy and put her on the cushion beside her.

Chrissy's gaze turned serious and Autumn felt a wave of nausea and knew that Chrissy was sending her information. The ground-level view showed the prone body of Gary Martin. Chrissy tucked into the crook of his arm nudging him, as he lay on his stomach, unmoving. A sound grabbed Chrissy's attention, and the point of view moved up to the open front door to see Alexis Davenport standing there, eyes large and her hand covering her mouth. She ran off and Autumn felt Chrissy's heart sink. The vision blurred and blanked out, leaving Autumn gasping for air at the sadness and the shock of what she had seen and felt.

Autumn hugged Chrissy tight and promised her that she was safe and that she would do everything she could to bring her daddy's killer to justice. They fell into a restless sleep.

⣾

A half hour later, the phone startled them awake. It was Ray with an update. Autumn wanted to talk in person to share what she had learned from Chrissy, but not over the phone. She also wanted to try the visioning trick with Ace to see if all dogs could do it, or just Chrissy. Ray and Ace arrived within the hour.

Ace walked in first to greet Chrissy. Ray stepped across the threshold, looking handsome in his gray pinstriped suit. He embraced Autumn as though they had not seen each other in ages. The warmth and strength of his body filled her with joy. He moved her inches from his body and looked into her glistening eyes. She smiled, letting him know she was ready. Their lips met in a gentle touch, their bodies melding one into the other.

As Ray pulled away, Autumn sighed and her eyes fluttered open.

"Just wanted to get that out of the way," said Ray, smiling.

He gave her a quick kiss and grabbed her hand. She led him into the living room, where Chrissy and Ace were happily going through the toy pile. A bottle of Chianti was breathing with two wine glasses at the ready. Autumn poured them each a healthy serving. Glass in hand, Ray updated Autumn about his conversation with Alexis.

"Do you think she's telling the truth?"

"I'm leaning toward that, but she still didn't report it. Odd behavior for someone who says she cared for the guy."

Autumn could not imagine leaving a loved one on the floor without calling for help.

"Is that a criminal offense?"

"There's no law in Pennsylvania, but in some other states there are laws called 'duty to rescue that says you have to help someone."

Autumn took a sip of wine and shook her head in disbelief.

"Either way, calling for help is just the right thing to do."

She took another sip of the calming grape. Someone had called 911 when she and her parents were in the accident. They had saved her life.

Ray held her hand, bringing her out of the memory. He and Chrissy were good at knowing when she started down the path of traumatic memories and pulling her back to center.

"I don't think she murdered Gary," said Autumn.

Ray repositioned himself on the couch, now fully facing her.

"What brings you to that conclusion?"

Her cell phone rang. Saved by the ringtone.

"Mind if I take this?"

Ray shook his head.

"Hey, stranger," said Stephanie.

"Hey, Steph. How's it going?"

"Good. Are you available for dinner?"

"Hold on a sec." She covered the mouthpiece with her hand.

"I'd love for you to meet my friend. How about we order in and all have dinner together."

"Sounds fine."

"Steph? Come on over and we can order in. There's someone I want you to meet."

"Another furry friend?"

They shared a laugh.

"Nope. Human this time."

"Oooh. Can't wait! Five o'clock?"

"Perfect." Then to Ray, "She'll be here at five. I'm glad you two get to meet."

"Me, too. I can tell a lot about a person by the company they keep." He wiggled his eyebrows up and down, making Autumn giggle. Then looked down at his suit. "I feel overdressed."

"You look positively dashing," said Autumn in her best impression of cliché royalty and kissed him on the cheek.

"Kisses don't get you off the hook, young lady. But I'll take it."

She squeezed his hand and waited a beat. "I want to share something with you and hope you can keep an open mind."

He frowned, then shook out his hands, cracked his neck, and gave a nod to continue. She smiled at how he enabled her to relax and share information that made her feel uncomfortable.

"It's about Chrissy."

Ray looked at Chrissy playing with Ace. "What about her?"

Autumn sighed. "She...shows me things."

"What kind of things?" He sat up straighter, listening.

It sounded crazy no matter how she presented it. Her hesitation made Ray put his arm around her shoulder.

"Chrissy, come here sweetheart."

Chrissy popped her head up from the squeaky toy she was sharing with Ace and trotted over to them. Autumn bent down, picked her up, and nestled her between Ray and herself.

"It's like a video, but shot from her point of view. Things a dog would observe."

"Like what?"

"Like Ace's friendly face dripping with drool from a lowered visual perspective, as it would look when Chrissy looks up at him."

Ray's face showed excitement and fascination rather than skepticism.

"I've had dogs all of my life. Dogs have their own special powers and ways of communicating. We don't understand the extent of them. Can she show me?"

Autumn stroked Chrissy's head and down her back, getting Chrissy's attention and making eye contact.

"Sweetheart, can you show Ray something like you show me?"

Chrissy grunted and turned to face Ray, who met her gaze. He felt queasy. Then the world swam and changed focus. His view was close to the floor, tugging on a blue stuffed doggy filled with squeakers, Ace pulling back on the other side. Chrissy made a *mrroww* sound and the nausea subsided as the vision faded. It took a moment to regain a sense of his own perspective. He looked at Autumn, mouth agape, not knowing what to say.

Autumn waited, knowing that the first time was the hardest. Stabilizing after a *Chrissy Vision*, as she now called them, required reorienting to the real world.

"Are you kidding me?" Ray put his hand to his head and then stared at Chrissy. She gave him one of her smiles and jumped off the couch to return to Ace.

Autumn was glad she had someone who shared the experience. It was hard keeping it to herself. She smiled at him.

"What did she show you?"

"Ace and her playing with the toy they're using right now." He looked over and had a different sense of the dogs' experience than ever before.

"Did you get nauseous?"

"Yes!"

"I think it's from the sudden shift in visual perspective. Almost like motion sickness."

Ray nodded, reaching for his wine. He took a gulp.

"Her ability is amazing. We could use it in all kinds of ways. People do things around dogs the same as if they were alone. She can show us that."

Autumn caught the "*us*" in his phrasing and liked the sound of it.

"Exactly. She shows me things about this case. The way her daddy passed and the people who saw the body."

"Tell me." Ray was in investigator mode.

"Corinne Taylor, who reported the body, stole Gary's watch and went through his pockets before calling emergency services. Alexis discovered the body first, but didn't touch it or cross the threshold. The door was open and Gary was on the floor, Chrissy next to him."

Ray's mind was reeling. He took notes as Autumn spoke.

"Can she show you the actual death?"

"She already has." She told Ray what Chrissy had shown her. "There was no one else there at the time of death."

Ray considered this.

"Having the visions is one thing. Proving it is another. So the question is how did the fentanyl get into his system?"

Autumn poured more wine into his glass, agreeing with Ray, relieved by his acceptance of Chrissy's ability.

"That I don't know." Autumn slid closer. "I haven't told anyone else about her."'

"Let's keep it that way. Our secret." Ray squeezed her hand.

"My best friend, Stephanie, senses Chrissy's needs, but didn't get a Chrissy Vision."

"Maybe it depends on how close the person is to Chrissy. I feel like we have a strong connection."

Autumn loved the sound of that.

"Chrissy is my first dog, so I have no source for comparison. Has Ace ever showed you a vision?"

"No, but then I never asked him to. I can sense what he wants or what he is trying to show me, but no visions. Let's see. Come here, boy!"

Ray patted his leg and Ace bounded over. He held Ace's face and gazed into his eyes, their faces close. "Show me something you've seen."

A minute passed. Ace held his stare, panted a few times, smiled, and licked Ray's face from chin to eye. Ray heard Autumn's laughter and giggled himself. He patted Ace and told him to go back to Chrissy.

"I guess Chrissy is unique," Autumn said between catching her breath between laughs.

"I guess so!" Ray wiped his face with a napkin.

᪲

Stephanie arrived with a chocolate bomb cake, decadent with thick chocolate fudge icing and a cool pudding center surrounded by dark chocolate cake. It was Autumn's weakness, worse than red licorice. She knew she would forgive Stephanie for derailing her healthy eating plan yet again. After all, dark chocolate was its own food group and said to be healthy. This was rationalization at its best.

Ray stayed in the living room, throwing a ball to Ace and Chrissy. The room was long and carpeted, allowing them to get traction as they ran and pounced on the ball. A lilting call to Chrissy sent her running into the foyer.

"Look what I have for a sweet little girl!" Stephanie squeezed a stuffed toy in the shape of a chipmunk.

124

Chrissy wagged her tail and accepted the toy, allowing Stephanie to scratch behind her ears, and then ran back in the living room to show Ace.

"Boy! No kiss or anything."

"Don't take it personally. She has a friend over." Autumn took the cake from Stephanie and walked into the kitchen.

"I thought you said you didn't get another dog?"

"I didn't. Ace is Ray's dog." Ray walked in on cue.

Startled at this handsome, well-built man, she stuttered a hello.

Ray gave her a dazzling smile and reached out to shake her hand.

"Nice meeting you."

"Ray, Stephanie. She's my best friend. Stephanie, Ray is the detective working on the case of Chrissy's pet parent and my…" She was at a loss as to how to describe their relationship.

Ray jumped in. "Boyfriend."

Autumn and Stephanie looked at him, eyes wide. Autumn's mouth opened in surprise. Ray put his arm around Autumn's waist.

"I hope it's not too soon to give me that title," he murmured in Autumn's ear and kissed the side of her head.

"Uh, no! No. It's fine." She smiled at him, glad he gave himself that designation, and then looked at Stephanie's shocked face.

"Another milestone in less than a week. I need to stay in touch daily to keep up with the news around here." She smiled. "You guys look good together."

Autumn loved hearing that. She was happier than she had been in months, maybe ever.

They all laughed. Tension broken, they ordered crab cake sandwich platters from the New Britain Pub. Autumn poured Stephanie a glass of wine and they all went into the living room for a relaxing evening of easy conversation and playing with the pups.

Autumn forgot to take her medication again.

⹀29⹀

The sun streamed through the circle top window and onto Autumn's face. She and Chrissy slept through the night after a happy evening with friends. It felt like old times in the house; so much laughter. Next to her, Chrissy blinked then stretched and yawned. She grabbed the little body and held her close, kissing the top of her head.

"I love you so much."

Chrissy grunted and licked Autumn's face.

They finished their morning routine, including taking Autumn's medication, just in time to receive Steve and Mickey.

"How are you feeling? Still on the pain meds?"

Steve chuckled. "Are you kidding? After the conversation we had with Julie? I talked to my doctor. He's weaning me off."

Autumn was glad to hear it. She liked Steve and felt protective of him as she would have with her own father. They made their way around several blocks, chatting about the weather, the neighbors' gardens, and the way the dogs were such good friends.

"My daughter is coming over to make lunch. Want to join us?"

"We'd love to. Lisa seems like a good cook, judging by the fragrance of her pasta sauce."

"Her mother's recipe. One o'clock?"

"See you then."

&O

They arrived on time with a lemon meringue pie and a bag of treats for Mickey. The fenced yard was a safe place to romp, and the furry friends had a blast with Mickey's toys and barking at squirrels, birds, and chipmunks.

Autumn watched Chrissy through the kitchen window while sipping on fresh-brewed iced tea. Lisa was scurrying about the kitchen, refusing help, so Steve and Autumn sat at the counter to keep her company. Lisa coated the complex salad of spring mix, fruits, seeds, and nuts with a light citrus dressing to accompany the pasta primavera topped with sauce made from white wine, garlic, and parmigiana cheese. Lisa pulled warm multigrain bread from the oven.

"This is wonderful, Lisa," Autumn said after chewing and swallowing a too-big forkful of pasta.

Lisa smiled. "Thank you. There were times when I thought about going to culinary school, but didn't want to lose my love of cooking. As a hobby is one thing, but as a job, it might become a chore."

"So you decided to become a legal assistant instead. What steered you in that direction?"

"The law fascinates me and I wanted something where I'd get to keep learning, although Vaughn isn't a very good teacher, and Gary was too focused on his own stuff to develop me."

"How about Fran? She's been doing the work longer. Could she provide some guidance?

Lisa accidentally spat out a bit of salad at the suggestion, choked, and drank some tea to clear her throat.

"Ha! That'd be the day. She thinks she knows everything but doesn't want to share."

"It's hard to work in the same space with difficult people," Steve offered.

"You're telling me!" Lisa chomped her food with a tight jaw.

"What is she like?"

Lisa put her fork down and wiped her mouth. "Infuriating. She withholds information I need, and kisses up to Vaughn. She even blamed me when Travis Mitchell threatened Gary."

Autumn continued eating, while Lisa vented.

"I overheard her talking to Vaughn about the missing funds from the Trust account. I told Gary, and he said he'd take care of it." She took a deep breath. "What if that's what got him killed?"

"Have you told the police about the embezzlement?" asked Steve, concerned about his daughter's involvement.

"No." She put her head in her hands.

"Maybe it's time," suggested Autumn.

"I don't want to get in trouble for obstruction of justice."

Autumn thought about Ray. "What if you could give a statement without worrying about that?"

"I guess that would be best. But how?"

"I have a friend on the force. Detective Ray Reed. He's a good guy."

"I know him. He's questioned Vaughn before." Lisa looked at her plate. "I'm wary of cops."

Steve put his hand on his daughter's arm. "It's better to tell him what you know. This has been eating at you."

She nodded her agreement. Autumn dialed Ray and asked him to come by Steve's house.

There was plenty of food to feed Ray, and his delight in Lisa's cooking made her relax. Also seeing Ace play with Mickey and Chrissy showed her another side of this particular detective. After being assured that she would not be in trouble in exchange for her statement, Lisa spilled the beans about Vaughn.

Lisa told Ray that Vaughn had stolen money from the Trust account. She emphasized that he should be disbarred. Finally, she expressed concern that Gary had confronted Vaughn about the embezzlement and lost his life because of it.

"Do you know if Vaughn had access to fentanyl?" Ray asked in a casual tone.

"Not sure. Travis Mitchell was a drug dealer and came to the office a lot. Who knows if he could have gone after Gary for losing his plea bargain?"

"Now, I have to ask this to be thorough. Did you have access to fentanyl, Ms. Coleman?"

Her breath hitched. "I wouldn't hurt Gary. I loved him."

"Please answer the question."

After a few beats, Steve jumped in. "I'm on fentanyl for surgical pain, but my daughter wouldn't have used it to hurt anyone."

"So you did have access?" Ray asked as gently as possible.

Lisa sighed. "Yes. But that doesn't mean I took it from Dad."

"Mr. Coleman, is any of your medication unaccounted for?"

"I'm pretty sure it's all there."

"Okay. We can confirm that later just for the record. Thanks for your cooperation."

Ray wrote everything down and then asked her to sign it as a formal statement. She did. He whistled for Ace and Autumn walked them to the door.

"Thanks for coming over. Strike while the iron is hot, right?"

"Right," he kissed her goodbye. "See you later?"

"I'd like that."

She watched him walk down the pathway feeling lucky.

It was time to serve dessert.

⸗30⸗

Ray and Ace had left a half hour ago and Autumn cleaned up from their visit. Chrissy whimpered at the back door. Autumn opened it, and Chrissy ran into the dark. She continued cleaning up. A few minutes went by and then too many more minutes. Autumn opened the door and called for Chrissy. She did not come.

Panicked, Autumn ran into the yard and called Chrissy. Nothing. Her heart pounded. Hyperventilating, she searched every corner of the yard. No sign of her. A half-hour went by. She called Steve and Julie in case Chrissy escaped to visit Mickey or Teddy. They had not seen her.

There came whimpering at the front door. Autumn flung it open. Chrissy lay on the front step, encased in a thin blanket bound tightly with twine, her little legs pinned to her body. She cried, unable to move. A note hung around her neck.

Let it go or you'll be sorry.

The note sent shivers up Autumn's spine. She cradled Chrissy and brought her inside, bolting the door behind them. She brought her fur baby to the couch and gently untied her.

"My poor sweetheart."

She unwrapped Chrissy and felt her legs and body. She checked for cuts and scrapes. Chrissy stood up and shook off.

"Oh thank goodness you're alright!"

Chrissy wagged her tail at Autumn.

"Show Mommy who did this to you."

A Chrissy Vision appeared of someone dressed in black, wearing a dark ski mask. This did not help identify the perpetrator.

Autumn dialed Ray, who said he was on his way back. She checked the locks on every door and window, and then cuddled Chrissy until Ray and Ace arrived.

"Are you okay?" Ray asked Autumn and Chrissy. "She wasn't able to identify who took her?"

"No. She showed me, but the person was covered up."

"You've been talking to a lot of people. Of those, who knows where you live?"

"Lisa Coleman and Fran Barnes, but it's easy enough to find my address online."

"True. You gave your name to Miranda Green, Corinne Taylor, Vaughn Evans, Anna Martin, and Alexis Davenport."

"They all seem to care about Chrissy, with the exception of Anna Martin. Why would they scare her?"

"The person was trying to scare you."

Autumn squeezed Chrissy in a protective hug.

"We have to get this person, Ray."

"The sooner the better. In the meantime, can you set us up in the living room? We're not leaving you alone tonight."

∞

The morning sun cleared the fear from the night before and replaced it with cautious determination. Ray and Autumn had breakfast on the patio while Ace sniffed along the fence line, alert to anything out of the ordinary. Chrissy followed him, observing.

Julie had called earlier to make sure Chrissy was back home. Steve and Mickey came at their usual time and had coffee while the pups played together in the yard.

"Thank goodness she was returned," said Steve.

"It was terrifying to have her go missing. It's my fault for letting her out back alone."

"There was no way you could know someone was lurking back there," said Ray.

"A motion-sensor floodlight is getting installed as soon as possible. No way Chrissy is allowed in the yard alone."

"What if you had been out there and ran into the person? There's no telling what they would have done to you."

"Steve makes an excellent point. I like the idea of motion-sensor lights out back. We can go to the home supply store and get a couple today. I'll put them in for you."

"What a bonus that you're handy." Autumn said.

"You have no idea. My electrical skills are only the tip of the iceberg." Ray winked and smiled.

"Let's take a lap around the block with these three before you head to the store. Then I'm going home to take a nap."

Ray whistled for the furry friends, who galloped over to the patio.

Autumn noticed that Steve seemed tired today. He only had one cup of coffee and slumped a little in his chair. She wondered if it had anything to do with coming off his medication.

⸗31⸗

Ray showed up at the law offices of Martin and Evans bright and early on Monday. Lisa sat at the first desk, and gave a cursory good morning then looked away. He approached Fran's desk. She received him with crossed arms and a scowl. Photos of her haughty cats adorned each corner of her desk amidst piles of paperwork. Their faces reminded him of Fran's own expression.

"I'm here to see Vaughn."

"He's busy right now."

"This isn't a request. Please let him know I'm here."

"C'mon, Kitty. Make it easy on everybody," said Lisa.

"Kitty?" Ray remembered the texts to and from Kitty on Gary's phone.

"Yeah, Fran is into cats, so we call her Kitty."

"Did Gary call you Kitty?"

"Yeah, what of it?"

"Can we speak privately?" asked Ray.

Fran gave him a dirty look and came out from behind her desk. She walked into the conference room. He shut the door behind them.

Arms crossed, Fran continued to display resistance.

"What were you and Gary texting about the night of his death?"

"How am I supposed to remember that?" The picture of a desert landscape on the wall behind Ray seemed to hold her attention.

"You two were trying to work something out. What was it?"

"None of your business."

"Actually it is, as long as this case is open."

Fran shuffled her feet and looked at the industrial gray and tan rug.

"Are you aware that three hundred thousand dollars is missing from the client Trust?"

"Yes. Gary took the money."

This conflicted with what Lisa said she had overheard.

"How do you know that?"

"Vaughn told me."

"And you trust his word?"

"All you need to know is that I wasn't there when Gary died."

"I'm going to need to know more than that. Where were you at the time of his death?"

"You said I was texting with him. Remember?"

"That could have been from anywhere, Ms. Barnes."

"Yeah, well I was still at the office."

"So you do remember texting with him. Why did he want you to go to his house?"

"Gary was in love with me. He wanted to talk about our relationship."

"What was the nature of your relationship?"

"I worked for his law firm. End of story. But he wanted more. Gary said he was tired of the dimwits he'd been hanging out with and wanted a woman of substance." Fran's chin lifted defiantly.

Ray had the sense that he was not going to get any more out of Fran Barnes today.

"Please let Vaughn know I'm here."

She left the room in a huff, Ray at her heels. He passed her in the reception area.

"No need to announce me."

He walked to Vaughn's office door, gave a quick knock, and walked in, leaving the door slightly ajar. Papers scattered across the desk, books lay open, and Vaughn clutched a handful of his own hair as he bent over the briefs.

Vaughn looked up from his paperwork and rolled his eyes.

"What now, Detective?"

"You look stressed."

"I have a complaint to submit in two hours. What do you want?"

"I have some new information I'd like to share with you."

"Such as?"

"I know it was you who embezzled the funds from the Trust account."

"You can't prove that."

"I have evidence that you had gambling debts in the same amount as the missing funds, and the videotape from the bank showing a withdrawal by you on the day the funds went missing."

"It was Gary, not me."

"Gary knew about it and threatened to contact the authorities. You would have been arrested and disbarred. How's that for a motive for murder?"

Vaughn pressed his lips together and pounded his fist on the desk.

"I didn't kill Gary!"

"You also had an affair with the victim's girlfriend, Miranda Green. Were you in love with her, Mr. Evans?"

"That chippy? I slept with her once to show Gary he wasn't the only guy who could get the girls."

"Your resentment toward the victim is showing. You're digging a hole for yourself."

Vaughn Evans closed his mouth.

"Mr. Evans, you're under arrest for suspicion of embezzlement and first degree murder. Will you come with me quietly or do we need to use the steel bracelets?"

Vaughn held his head in his hands, shaking it left to right as Ray read his Miranda rights, the irony of the name of these rights and Vaughn's affair with Miranda not lost on either of them. Fran was at the filing cabinet nearest to Vaughn's door, fists clenched. Ray wondered how long she had been standing there and what she had overheard.

Lisa and Fran watched in worried silence as Ray led Vaughn from his office. He didn't make eye contact when he asked Fran to call his attorney.

=32=

The news that Vaughn Evans was arrested on suspicion of embezzlement and the murder of Gary Martin traveled through the small town of Knollwood. Miranda Green sipped her morning latte when the story blasted out of her television and stabbed her in the stomach. Could her affair with Vaughn implicate her in some way? Would she be questioned about his crimes and her possible collusion in Gary's death?

Her next swallow of coffee was cold. She had not realized the news put her into shock long enough for the piping hot beverage to chill. Maybe it was time to take a vacation until this storm blew over. No one would have known about the affair if she had not blabbed it to that woman who now had Chrissy. What was her name? She could find out easy enough. Then what? Threaten her not to tell anyone?

She paced the tile floor of her kitchen. Even her view of the condominium complex's pool and beautiful garden did nothing to calm her nerves. She pictured Vaughn as he spilled his guts about their private conversations. It made her stomach churn. She tried to remember all the things they'd shared out of anger, fantasizing about Gary's permanent removal from the planet. Turns out, he was more trouble dead than alive.

The anger she had felt when she found out about Alexis was enough to make her think about ending not only their relationship but his life, as well. No one gets the better of Miranda Green! After giving it more thought, she had decided that getting him back through Vaughn was a better plan. That would upset Gary more than Miranda's departure. She knew he would easily replace her.

Vaughn proved to be as vindictive as she was. He not only cheated with Gary's girlfriend, he stole from the practice. Gary never promised her exclusivity, so it turned out that with all of Gary's issues, he had more integrity than Vaughn did. It had never been the same after she slept with Vaughn. She could not look at Gary without experiencing guilt and wished she had never succumbed to temptation and resentment.

She placed a call to her travel agent and booked herself on the first cruise out of Bayonne, New Jersey, which happened to be leaving the next day. Last minute reservations were great, since she saved a bundle on the room. She had not been to New England and Nova Scotia, but more important, it was away where she could think what to do next and evade questioning by the police.

⚡33⚡

Autumn and Chrissy were on their morning walk when they spotted Julie and Teddy half a block away. Chrissy barked in greeting and Teddy replied. Julie waited until they caught up, then they continued their stroll.

"Did you hear about Vaughn Evans?" said Julie.

"What about him?"

"He was arrested for embezzlement and the murder of Gary Martin."

Autumn stopped short. Ray did not mention this to her, and she felt betrayed. She shook off her anger and responded.

"Do you think he did it?"

"Well, theft is his motive. And he was often with the victim or knew his schedule, giving him ample opportunity."

Autumn considered these points.

"Could be. But what about Travis Mitchell?"

"Maybe Travis knew about the murder and threatened Vaughn with the information?"

"Hmmm." Autumn thought the idea made sense, but something still seemed out of place. She needed to talk to Ray, if for nothing else, to find out why he had left her out of the loop.

∞

Autumn disregarded Dr. Wes' guidance about waiting before acting when anger or panic rose, as she pounded her phone's contacts. How dare Ray ignore her? She felt excluded.

"I can't tell you every time I make an arrest!" Ray defended himself.

Autumn gripped the phone, trying to get control of herself.

"How do you think it made me feel to hear the news from Julie?"

There was silence on the other end of the line.

"Did you hear me? It was even on the news!" Her chest heaved.

An audible sigh met her argument.

"Listen, I can't talk about this right now. I'll call you later."

She heard a click. Staring at the phone, Autumn broke down in tears. Shaking, she took her morning dose of medication. What had she been thinking? How could this relationship be different from the others?

∞

The air was tense between the women's desks made worse by the absence of Vaughn and Gary. They had barely spoken since Vaughn's arrest. Fran blamed Lisa for blabbing. Lisa did not want to get into it, so she kept her head down and focused on paperwork. Finally, the stress made Fran blow.

"Where do you get off telling that detective that Vaughn took the money?"

"It's true, isn't it?" Lisa blurted.

"You don't know anything about anything. This is all Gary's fault, and he paid for it with his life."

Lisa started crying.

"What a baby you are." Fran had no sympathy.

Lisa's tears flowed, her breaths short but soundless.

꿍

Ray felt restless after his conversation with Autumn. He had already let his guard down too many times on this case. He trusted her, but had to withhold certain information to ensure the integrity of the evidence. Not even the press had details of Vaughn's arrest.

Taken aback by Autumn's reaction, he wondered if he had hurt their relationship. Maybe he had jumped in too fast. Maybe they were not meant to be after all.

꿍

Two hours later, Autumn had not moved from the sofa, where she hugged an oversized pillow. Chrissy stared at her from the floor after trying to nudge, bark, and growl Autumn out of her funk. Silent tears dripped down her face and her mind flashed her conversation with Ray. Worry blossomed and filled every fiber of her being.

They had spent a beautiful weekend together. They held hands as they walked the pups and snuggled on the couch watching movies, comfortable in each other's arms. They had not talked about the case at all. It felt right and easy to be together. So why did this one omission send her into a tailspin? Had she pushed him too far? Did she have the right to demand information from him?

A moan escaped her mouth and Chrissy turned her head to the side, wondering what the sound meant. She returned it with a one-bark vocalization and blinked at Autumn, who stared blankly past her. Chrissy lay down and put her head on her paws, staring up at Autumn every few minutes.

Autumn felt herself sinking deeper, losing ground from the progress she had made over the last few weeks. The darkness of love lost and hope smashed overwhelmed her, taking her purpose and meaning with it.

136

Dr. Wes popped into her mind. *Challenge these thoughts.* She grasped her thoughts and twisted them by asking different questions of herself. Had she been unfair to Ray? He must have a good reason for not telling her. Was it time to explore her reaction with Dr. Wes? That was enough to lift her head out of the hole and acknowledge Chrissy. She reached down to pet her. Chrissy stood and met her hand, then jumped on the couch and settled next to her.

Pulling out of an anxiety death spiral was never easy. She gave herself kudos for only staying in it for a couple of hours. She instead decided to beat herself up for being hard on Ray.

Chrissy stared at Autumn, and a wave of nausea overcame her. She found herself looking up at Ray's broad smile, a flash of their clasped hands from an eye-level perspective – Chrissy's eye level, that is. She felt the connection through Chrissy's doggy senses. She saw Ray's hand reach down and pet Chrissy's head, and felt Chrissy's happiness. The image closed and Chrissy wagged her tail.

"You like him as your new daddy?" Autumn hoped that was still a possibility.

Chrissy beat her tail against the floor.

Autumn would wait for him to call her.

In the meantime, she wanted to think about the case. She wondered what prompted Ray to arrest Vaughn rather than digging for more information.

≈34≈

The underground parking garage of Miranda's building was quiet except for her high heels clicking against the pavement. Most of the residents were at work, so her car sat alone. Bags packed with some summer attire plus sweaters for chilly New England evenings on the water, she looked forward to a change of scene and time to relax. Miranda put her rolling suitcase and carry-on bag into the trunk of her BMW.

Clicking the key fob to unlock the door, she lifted the car door handle, slid into the driver's seat, and reached for her seatbelt. A sharp pain in her chest caused her to stop the motion. Her breath caught. She gasped for air. Unable to pull in oxygen, her lips went numb. The last thing she saw was the stenciled number on the column that indicated her condominium address.

∞

Lisa Coleman took a walk at lunch, needing to get away from the toxic hatred emanating from Fran. The anger spilled out like lava with burning remarks if Lisa made the smallest sound and erupted like a volcano in the form of accusations of Lisa's stupidity triggered by the simplest questions about work.

She tried to be compassionate and wondered if it was Fran's worry for Vaughn. They did not know the length of his incarceration. It felt odd that a criminal defense attorney could not get himself out of jail. Even if they released Vaughn on bail, there was no guarantee that he would be allowed to practice law until the case was resolved.

Concerned about a possible office shutdown, Lisa considered her options. Giving up her apartment would be disappointing, but her dad would not mind if she came home for a while. Her stint as a legal assistant showed her how difficult the legal profession was. The constant search for cases and the type of people criminal attorneys dealt with did not appeal to her. Maybe she could work for a corporate attorney. The thought produced sadness rather than excitement.

More than anything, she wanted to feel happy about her work and do it in a way that made others happy. It was obvious that she did not make Fran bubble over with joy, and the clients did not value her contribution to their cause. Decision made, she headed back to the office.

∞

Fran sat at her desk, stewing. Her dedication to Vaughn had gone unnoticed and that infuriated her. The late nights, the devotion, watching his back and making sure he was taken care of – none of it mattered. And that wench Miranda sleeping with him on top of everything else. How dare Vaughn pull something like that?

She pounded on her desk, shaking the frames holding photos of her beloved cats. Cats are the only trustworthy creatures, she thought. She picked up the photos of Gabby and Sissy, kissing them in turn. If something happened to her, who would take care of them?

Chrissy had found a home, so why not her precious felines? That busybody, Autumn, stirred things up. All those questions. Everything was fine until she started coming around with Chrissy.

She let out a primal scream and banged her fist on the desk again, wishing she had a punching bag with Gary's face on it. This was all his fault, after all.

∞

Lisa entered the lobby of the office building. Her hand on the knob, she heard banging and yelling penetrating the door. She pushed the door open and peeked into the office as a projectile came whistling toward her, just missing her head. She slammed the door shut and made a beeline for her car. Safely in its cabin, she wasted no time in pulling out and heading for home, vowing never to return.

She pulled into her dad's driveway, hoping he was home. Lisa used her key to enter the house. Mickey barked and came running. Lisa reached out to pet him and he pulled away and barked turning for her to follow.

"Dad?"

No reply.

"Dad?"

She tried a little louder, but nothing. His car was in the driveway and Mickey was home, so he had to be in the house. Mickey led her to the master bedroom. She found him, unresponsive, on the floor next to his bed.

"Dad!"

She dialed 911.

∞

Autumn and Chrissy had just started their walk when they saw the ambulance pull up in front of Steve Coleman's house. They broke into a run. Lisa was at the door, hurrying the emergency medical techs into the house. She looked up and waved the pair in, not waiting for them before turning to lead the EMTs to her father.

They crossed the threshold and waited for Lisa to come back. Chrissy let out a sad bark that brought Mickey out of the bedroom. They nuzzled each other and Mickey sat, his mouth downturned and head lowered. Autumn petted his head and reassured him that his daddy would be okay. At least she hoped that was true, knowing things did not always turn out the way you wished they would.

The paramedics brought Steve out on a stretcher, an oxygen mask on his face. Lisa stood behind the gurney biting her nails.

"We'll take Mickey back to our house. You go ahead with your dad." Autumn spotted a pad and pen. "Here's my number. Please keep us posted."

Lisa nodded and they left the house together. Lisa locked the door behind her and followed the ambulance in her car. Autumn watched them pull away, sending good wishes after them. She looked down at her charges.

"How about a nice walk?"

They looked up at her, eyes glistening.

"It'll be okay. One trip around the block, and then we'll get something to eat."

Chrissy pushed against Mickey, encouraging him to walk. They took off down the street, worry slowing their pace. Autumn pulled out her cell and dialed Stephanie, hoping she could come over and wait for news of Steve's condition.

&

Stephanie got there as soon as she could, having stopped home to change after work and pick-up Italian hoagies with extra hot peppers, on the way over. Chrissy and Mickey greeted her at the door, interested in what was in the bag. They followed her into the kitchen.

"How are you holding up?"

"I'm worried that I haven't heard from Lisa."

"You know how hospital emergency rooms are. They need to figure out what's wrong, and that could take a while."

Autumn nodded, unwrapping her hoagie. The scent of olive oil and hot peppers reminded her that she had not eaten and neither had the fur babies.

"Let me feed these two, and then we can eat."

She put out the food in two separate bowls with their own water. They got along well and had no food aggression issues with one another. They ate peacefully with Mickey picking at his food more than Chrissy.

Autumn understood his reluctance to eat. She had lost her appetite over a fight with Ray, let alone something as serious as a health issue.

Stephanie and Autumn ate in silence, despite the perfect blend of meat and cheese on a fresh roll.

"So how's it going with Ray?"

Autumn's chewing slowed. After a few beats she looked at Stephanie. "Not sure."

"Why not?"

"I kind of yelled at him."

"About what?"

"He arrested Vaughn and didn't tell me."

Stephanie's questioning eyebrow went up. Autumn looked down. "I know. Stupid."

"Not stupid, just presumptuous. He's got a job to do."

"Yeah."

They took a few more bites of hoagie.

"Do you think he'll call?" Autumn asked.

Stephanie nodded, wiping her mouth. "If the night I met him is any indication, something like this won't dissuade him."

"I hope you're right."

As if the hoagies did not contain enough calories, Autumn broke out the Ben & Jerry's Chunky Monkey, making it necessary to take a longer evening walk than usual. Stephanie helped by walking Mickey and offering encouragement and optimism about Autumn's future with Ray.

They all sat on the couch when the call came in from Lisa. Autumn put it on speaker.

"He's stable," she said, the relief in her voice palpable.

"Thank goodness!" Autumn said, relieved as well.

Stephanie smiled at the news.

"The fentanyl caused an abnormal heart rhythm and decreased oxygen levels. They are working to get him off it as soon as possible and manage the damage it caused. The doctor is optimistic."

Autumn sighed. More problems from fentanyl use.

"Well, he's in the right place to get treatment. Please tell him that Mickey is fine and can stay with us for as long as he needs to."

"Thanks. That's a relief."

"Chrissy enjoys having her friend here. I know that Mickey is a therapy dog. Is it okay to bring him to see Steve?"

"He in intensive care right now. When they move him, hopefully sometime tomorrow, then you can bring Mickey."

"We'll wait to hear from you."

The following afternoon, they had a surprise visit from Julie and Teddy. Mickey and Chrissy welcomed Teddy and the three went to play in the den while the women drank iced tea in the kitchen.

"I couldn't believe it when they brought Miranda in," said Julie shaking her head. "What is this world coming to?"

"What happened?" Autumn felt alarm building in her chest.

"Someone in her complex found her dead in the car. My friend at the morgue told me she'd been there overnight."

"What did she die from?"

"That's the crazy part." Julie waited a few beats to build drama. Her eyebrows went up. "Fentanyl poisoning."

"First Gary, then Travis, and now Miranda. There must be a connection. No way this is just a rash of fentanyl overdoses."

"I agree, but what do they have in common?"

"The question might be *who* do they have in common?"

"Vaughn was in jail last night, so there's no way he could have done it."

"Unless he paid someone to do it or did it before his arrest. He had an affair with Miranda. Maybe he was afraid she would say something about Gary's death."

"Vaughn knew all three of the victims." Julie chewed her lip, puzzling out the problem.

"We have a motive for him with Miranda and Gary."

"Why would he kill Gary?"

"Jealousy? Anger over the embezzled funds?"

"I thought Ray arrested Vaughn for taking the money."

"I did."

Autumn spun around. Chrissy's tail wagged rapidly and she let out a few high-pitched squeaks in greeting.

"You don't seem happy to see me." Ray said from a few feet away. "At least Chrissy is."

Ray walked over and petted her. "Hi, hi, hi," he said in rhythm to her tail.

He stood up and faced Autumn. Ace and Chrissy joined Mickey and Teddy in the den.

Julie broke the silence. "Did you hear about Miranda Green?"

"Yeah. We had to let Vaughn go on the murder charge. The embezzlement hearing is pending, but he's been released."

Autumn looked down, not speaking as a safeguard against saying the wrong thing.

Julie excused herself, saying she had to get home before Brad left for work. She touched Autumn's arm.

"Call me later?"

Autumn nodded. She knew the abrupt exit was out of courtesy.

"Want some iced tea?" Autumn offered.

"Sure. Thanks."

They drank in silence for a couple of minutes and listened to birds chirping.

"Ace seems kind of tired."

"He is. We've been working around the clock on this case, and he needs some rest. Actually, I could use some myself, but couldn't sleep until we cleared the air."

A pang of guilt hit Autumn.

"I'm sorry," she said. Her sadness threatened to overwhelm her.

Ray stopped and lifted her chin with his forefinger.

"I know this is all new for you. It is for me too. I don't have the best track record with relationships, so let's figure some things out together."

She looked at him with glistening eyes, a single tear escaping down her cheek. He wiped it away.

"If we're going to move forward, we need to talk about boundaries when it comes to police business."

Autumn nodded, glad for the chance to start again.

Ray slid his hand into hers. Their fingers entwined, hope for the future was restored.

⸗36⸗

Autumn opted for the couch in Dr. Wes's office rather than the chair. She felt a bit beaten up and the deep cushions comforted her. Chrissy snuggled against her leg.

Doctor Wes peered at Autumn. Slumped on the couch, she held Chrissy close.

"How have things been going with Ray?"

Autumn closed her eyes.

"He's so understanding. I don't deserve it."

"Why not?"

She took a breath. "I almost ruined it."

"What happened?"

Autumn told him about their tiff and that Ray came over to mend things. Doctor Wes nodded as he listened.

"What do you make of his gesture?"

"That he's a good man who cares about me...and about Chrissy."

"What are you feeling about your own behavior?"

Autumn shook her head, mouth turned down. "What's wrong with me? He has a job to do. Getting angry with him for doing his job isn't right."

"Have you both come to some ground rules about that?"

"Yes. We talked about it, and now I know that he wasn't cutting me out of the case. But I just reacted! I didn't think!" She wrung her hands.

"From what you've told me, Ray isn't holding that against you. Going forward, let's talk about ways you can catch yourself before going into that same territory."

"Okay."

"What happened right before you had the argument?"

"I heard about Vaughn's arrest on the news and from a neighbor rather than from him."

"What thoughts went through your mind?"

"That he cut me out. I felt ignored and excluded. Like he didn't care."

"And the truth of the situation?"

"He does care, more than I realized. My expectations and his actions didn't align."

"Sounds like you were feeling insecure about the relationship."

"I was…I am, but Ray took the time to explain the situation at work rather than dismissing my concerns. Even though he was exhausted from being on duty, he wanted to make sure we were solid before he took time for himself. It meant a lot to me."

"The selflessness of his action, the way he put you first."

"Yes, that's it. I have more faith in it now. I want to work on controlling my reaction so I don't turn him off with my insecurity."

"When you snapped at him, where did you feel it in your body?"

"My heart. It felt tight and heavy."

"Could that relate to your worry of being abandoned? Having your heart broken again?"

"I'm sure it does. That makes sense."

"Next time you start feeling your heart getting tight and heavy, feel your feet on the ground…"

"I'm a champ at that strategy."

Doctor Wes smiled. "And then take a deep breath and let out all of the tension before speaking. The trigger will be the heaviness in your chest."

Autumn took a breath. "Good plan. I'll try that."

"How have you been doing with your medication?"

"I missed a dose, but I'm still taking it twice a day. Can we lessen the dose?"

"Okay." Dr. Wes wrote some instructions and handed them to Autumn. "We'll cut the dose in half to start with."

Autumn liked the sound of that.

"How have you and Chrissy been getting along?"

"She was kidnapped and returned. It made me realize how much I love her."

"Kidnapped?"

"We don't know who took her, but they were warning me off the case."

"What steps are you taking to ensure your safety?"

"I don't take my eyes off her. Ray installed motion-sensor lights, and I've stopped questioning suspects."

"Letting Ray handle it, yes?"

"Yes."

"Is Chrissy still helping with your anxiety?"

"She's my saving grace. She has a way of bringing me out of a funk."

"Good! Is there anything else that's top of mind?"

"My neighbor. He's in the hospital. It made me think of my dad. I hope he'll be okay. I feel bad for his daughter, Lisa. We're watching Mickey while he's recovering."

"You've taken one worry from their plate by taking care of Mickey. How is Chrissy reacting to that?"

"She loves having Mickey there, but doesn't want him on the bed with us." Autumn smiled. "He's a good boy, and I wanted to do something to help."

"The need to help is part of your nature. It might have contributed to your reaction to Ray. You want to help Chrissy. That's the other layer to the situation with Ray. Besides feeling left out, you interpreted his actions as preventing you from working on the case and helping Chrissy."

Autumn brightened. "That's true. I never thought about it that way."

"Whenever you have a reaction to something or set a goal, take stock of your intention in that circumstance. Align your behaviors, thoughts, and feelings with that intention rather than with what you expect from others. This creates stability and allows you to maintain your focus."

"That makes so much sense. Be mindful of my intention." She wrote it in her pocket notebook. Looking at Chrissy, she said, "Keep me on track, sweetheart."

Chrissy looked up and smiled.

⸗37⸗

Steve lay in his private room at the hospital, watching television. His cardiologist decided to keep him for the week to ensure the crisis had passed. He was glad that Lisa could stay with him for most of the day and into the evening. She was good company. He knew that his wife would have done the same if she were alive.

"Dad?"

"Yes, dear."

"I've been doing a lot of thinking."

"About what?"

"My life. Your life. Mom's life. Gary's life. It's all too short, isn't it?"

"Well, making the most of the time we have is a good idea."

"That's why I decided to leave my job."

Steve turned off the television, giving Lisa his full attention.

Lisa continued. "I realized that being miserable isn't how I want to live my life. With Gary gone, I have no reason to stay in my current job. Heck, there may not be a job to go back to. Even if there was, Fran is such a nasty person. Sitting across from her is hell."

"What are your plans?"

"I was hoping to take some time to figure it out. In the meantime, I'd like to move in with you and take care of you and Mickey."

A smile crept over Steve's face.

"You sure you want to live with your old man?"

"You're not that old. Besides, I want to make sure you're fine."

"I'd love to have you come home. The house feels empty without you."

Lisa went over to the bed and hugged her father over the array of intravenous and oxygen tubes.

଼

Autumn, Chrissy, and Mickey walked into the hospital lobby and up to the visitor's desk. Chrissy wore her pink emotional support animal vest and Mickey had his therapy dog tag credentials. Being in the hospital was no fun for Steve, and Mickey was depressed without his daddy, so it was time for a visit.

Steve's face brightened when he saw Mickey, reaching for him from behind the tangle of tubes. Mickey trotted over and put his head on the bed so Steve could reach him. His tail wagged as glad to see Steve as Steve was to see him. Lisa patted his back.

"What a great surprise!" Lisa said.

"Mickey missed his daddy, and we wanted to visit, too."

"I haven't seen Dad smile like this since he's been here. Thanks for coming."

Autumn was happy to see that their visit lifted Steve's spirits.

"When do you get to come home?"

"I have to stay the rest of the week. Doctor's orders. Hopefully, they'll let me out of here by Friday, but I plan to convince them that I'm well enough to leave sooner than that." Steve's hand never left Mickey.

"I'll be moving into the house to take care of him."

"What about work?"

"I've decided not to go back. I can't stand being near Fran, and I'll bet Vaughn plans to cut my job. I haven't heard anything about getting a new attorney to replace Gary."

"Vaughn has other things on his mind right now," said Autumn.

"Yeah, being arrested and all. I can't expect him to make any major decisions right now. If they find him guilty, the whole practice would shut down. That'd leave Fran out in the cold," Lisa said. Her clenched jaw and cold grin showed Autumn the strain Lisa had been under.

"My dad used to say that things tend to work out for the best. Whatever justice is waiting for Vaughn, his guilt or innocence in Gary's murder and client trust embezzlement, at least you'll be away from that situation," said Autumn.

"That's right. Knowing I don't have to go back there on Monday makes me feel calmer already."

"And knowing you'll be there when I get out of here makes me feel better," Steve said with a smile.

∞

Back at home, Autumn wiped down counters and the outdoor furniture to disperse the restlessness while she waited for Ray's arrival. The cloth came away with yellow pollen. She didn't want to make the same mistakes, and her anxiety elevated the chance of saying the wrong thing.

The doorbell rang, and Chrissy went running, her high-pitched welcome voice signaling Ray and Ace. Chrissy's accuracy at knowing who was at the door still surprised Autumn. Maybe it had to do with her keen sense of smell.

Wiping her hands on a clean dishcloth, Autumn went to answer the door. Chrissy's tail wagged at full speed, welcoming her two friends.

Ray stepped across the threshold and Ace ran past him to sniff Chrissy. Ray gave Autumn a light kiss on the mouth and grinned at her.

"Something smells good."

"It's a tuna casserole. I haven't made it in a long time. It was the one thing my mom said I made better than anyone."

Ray followed her into the kitchen and watched her check their lunch in the oven. She poured him some iced tea and put fresh mint sprigs in the glass, trying not to splash any on the counter. He took a sip.

"Fresh brewed is the best."

"The mint is from my mother's garden. It comes back every year."

Ray put down his glass and folded his hands in his lap.

"We need to talk."

Autumn's heart pounded. Anxiety flooded her mind, her fears colliding, turning into a dark coil of emotional pain. Her breath was short, only reaching the bottom of her throat.

Ray saw her panic rise. "Whoa, wait a minute!"

Autumn fell into a kitchen chair, barely hearing him. Chrissy ran over, barking and pushing against her leg. The barking got through the jumble of despair, growing louder as she came out of her attack. She reached down and grabbed Chrissy, holding her close, breathing in her earthy scent, and focusing on her silky ears. Hugging her warm body made Autumn feel grounded again. She regained her senses and felt her feet on the floor. Ray had put a glass of iced tea in front of her. She had not noticed it until now. She took a sip, her breathing calmed, and her mind focused on his face looking for clues as to the topic of what they had to talk about.

Ray slid his chair close and put his palm on her thigh.

"Everything's okay."

"Is it?" She gave Chrissy a lingering hug. Chrissy pressed her cheek against Autumn's head. "Even now that you know I'm crazy?"

Ray shook his head. "You don't get it."

"Get what? That I'm too damaged to be in a relationship?"

Ray gave a weak smile. "No. That we're more alike that you realize."

Autumn frowned, not being able to imagine Ray having a panic attack.

"I told you that I have a little PTSD myself. I'm a U.S. Marine veteran. Served in Afghanistan. Without going into detail, I saw some things that put me over the edge for a while. Had full blown PTSD."

Autumn's eyes widened. "You seem so...normal."

Laughing, he squeezed her thigh. "How do you define normal? But seriously, I got the help I needed and went through a specialized program for veterans."

"Does it ever happen now? Your panic attacks, I mean."

"Sometimes, but less and less. Certain things can trigger it, but I've got control over it for the most part. Ace helps me like Chrissy helps you."

Autumn nodded. "So there's hope for me."

"No doubt about it. And Chrissy and I are here to help."

He reached around Autumn with a gentle hug, not pressing too hard so as not to crush Chrissy who still clung to Autumn's chest. Looking into her eyes, he said, "I'm not going anywhere."

She let out the breath she did not realize she had been holding and felt her chest lighten, thankful for this revelation and for having love and support in her life.

=38=

Fran sat at her desk, moving papers around, feeling distracted, when Vaughn strode through the door. She had mixed feelings about his return. After all, her devotion to him had gone unnoticed and his desire earned Miranda his physical affection. She was not sure if she could sway his emotions in her direction.

"Fran! Good to see you." Vaughn glanced at Lisa's empty desk.

"She quit."

Vaughn frowned at the curt reply.

"Did she say why?"

"Nope. Just got up the other day and didn't come back."

Vaughn's plans for the practice were up-in-the-air anyway, so he felt relieved having one less person to pay.

"Are you planning to stick around?"

"Depends."

"On what?"

She pursed her lips. "On you."

"I'm planning to stay out of jail, but if I get convicted of embezzlement, I'll be disbarred."

"And I lose my job."

"Your concern is overwhelming."

She sniffed. "You have no idea how I've protected you all this time, and look at the thanks I get."

"What does that mean? You know I appreciate the work you do for me."

"Is that all I am to you? Your tireless worker?"

The pitch of her voice grew more intense.

"I don't know what you're talking about." Vaughn started toward his office door.

Fran picked up one of the ceramic cats on her desk and threw it, hitting him squarely in the back. Vaughn turned, anger filling his face and his voice.

"What's your problem?"

"You're my problem!" She was on the verge of screaming.

Vaughn shook his head, weary from being in jail and not in the mood for Fran's tirade.

"Look, I'm exhausted and have more problems right now than I can handle. Can I get a little support?"

"I've done nothing but support you. Gary didn't. Lisa didn't. Miranda didn't."

"What do they have to do with you?"

"They have everything to do with you!"

Fran's eyes were wild.

Vaughn backed away from her.

"Listen, I have to take care of a few things before all hell breaks loose." Vaughn turned, went to his office, and closed the door.

Fran stood at her desk, seething, vowing that all hell would break loose, and she would be the one to launch it. How dare Vaughn dismiss her? She loved him almost as much as she loved her cats. He didn't see it. He didn't care. She gathered her purse and slammed the door behind her on the way to her car.

Vaughn sat in his office, head in hands. He jumped when the door slammed but was relieved that Fran had departed. He didn't need another problem right now. It was just as well. He would be closing the office and heading for his Moroccan getaway using a false passport.

⇗39⇗

Autumn and Chrissy were taking their evening stroll. The misty air and light fog gave the neighborhood a murky appearance. With Lisa Coleman staying at her dad's, Mickey was back home. They expected Stephanie, Ray, and Ace for dinner soon, so this would be a short walk.

A streetlight up ahead showed the figure of a woman wearing a scarf and a raincoat, her hands hidden in her pockets. As they approached the woman, she called out to them.

"Did you think you could catch me?"

Autumn squinted to see who it was and decided to stop where they were. The woman walked toward them.

"Who is it?"

Chrissy's low growl became more urgent with each step the woman took.

"Shut that dog up!"

Autumn gathered Chrissy in her arms and started back toward her house.

"Don't take another step!" the woman shrieked.

Chrissy blasted her with a series of angry barks; Autumn wasn't sure what to do.

"Who are you?"

"You couldn't let it alone, could you?"

"Fran?"

"Everything was going fine until you stuck your nose in."

"But Chrissy, her daddy..."

"Yeah, that darn Chrissy. Wasn't the warning I left around Chrissy's neck enough for you?"

"You're the one who kidnapped Chrissy! How could you?" Autumn turned away to put Chrissy out of range of this lunatic.

"You had me over to your house to find out more about Gary's death. Nice try. And I overheard your conversation with Vaughn when you came to the office."

A light bulb turned on in Autumn's head. "You killed Gary. But how?" Autumn tried to keep her talking.

"When I put the fentanyl powder on the doorknob, I made sure that there was none on the ground, to protect Chrissy. I should've made sure to include her. My own stupid fault for making sure it didn't touch her."

Autumn clutched Chrissy, horrified at the thought of Fran murdering this sweet little pup.

"Gary was the one who had to go. He wanted to turn Vaughn in for stealing the money. I couldn't let him do that. Then Travis. How could he threaten me after I slept with him to get the fentanyl I needed?" she screamed.

"You put the powder in Travis's pocket?"

"Of course! He was a drug dealer, but he wasn't stupid enough to touch the stuff himself."

"You did what you felt was necessary." Autumn tried to sound understanding. It took all the bravery she could muster.

"What would you know? How could Vaughn have an affair with Miranda, knowing how I felt about him? I loved him; she didn't. I had to do something about her, too."

Autumn gasped. Fran had committed three murders in the name of love. Fran's hateful grin would haunt Autumn for a long time. If she lived past tonight.

"How did you kill Miranda?"

"Same way as the others. Put fentanyl powder on her car door handle. It was just a matter of time."

Autumn could feel Chrissy shaking.

"And now it's your turn."

Fran pulled her hand out of her pocket to reveal a gun.

"You don't want to do that Ms. Barnes," Ray's calm voice came from Autumn's right. She didn't know if her terror had distracted her from noticing or if he was that quiet when he walked. The gun in his right hand pointed at Fran while his left gently guided Autumn and Chrissy behind him.

"Ray! Thank God!"

"I'm tired of people telling me what I want and don't want," Fran said, moving the gun up and down for emphasis.

"Please, Ms. Barnes. No one wants to get hurt."

Fran fired the gun. The shot went past Ray's head and whizzed by Autumn, who held Chrissy close with her hand protecting the soft, furry head. The sound of deep, frantic barking preceded Ace bounding down the street. Fran tried to fire again, but the gun jammed, giving Ace enough time to pounce and pin her to the ground. The gun flew from her hand. Ace bared his teeth over her face and growled. She did not move.

Ray called in for a squad car. Within moments, a police car pulled up, the emergency lights flashing red and blue against the houses on either side of the street. The officer jumped out of the car, his gun pointed at Fran. Her hands were already up, threatened by Ace.

Ray walked over to Ace.

"Good boy! Let her up now."

Ace stood over her for another moment, teeth bared and saliva dripping, and then backed next to Ray.

Fran looked to ensure Ace was no longer a threat before moving. The officer grabbed her arm and yanked her to her feet. Neighbors came out to see what was going on, including Lisa Coleman. They watched as the officer cuffed Fran Barnes.

"Fran? What's going on?" Lisa asked.

"You're so naïve, Lisa." She spat on the sidewalk in Lisa's direction.

Lisa ran over to Autumn and Chrissy; Mickey barked from the window.

"You okay?" Lisa asked.

They stood in place, shaking. Autumn hugged Chrissy to comfort them both. Ray walked over and put his arms around them. Autumn felt his warmth melting the chill and the shock. Ace stood by, protecting them all.

Chrissy mewled, suffocated by the shows of affection. Autumn put her on the sidewalk and she shook out her long hair and sat next to Ace. They sniffed each other in greeting, glad it was over.

"Everything is alright now," Ray told Autumn and Lisa.

Julie and Teddy ran up the street. Autumn looked up and smiled, the odd thought that even when she was running, Julie's hair stayed in place. Teddy checked on Chrissy, his short tail at attention. Julie put her hand on Autumn's shoulder, head shaking at seeing Fran loaded into the police car.

"I'm sorry I brought her to your house! I put you in danger," Julie cried.

"It wasn't your fault." Autumn touched Julie's hand. To Ray, she said, "Can her confession be used?"

"Yes," said Ray. "She gave it voluntarily. She was not under arrest at the time. I heard part of it, but you are the primary witness. I'll need to take a formal statement from you."

"No problem," said Autumn. "Boy, talk about getting what you ask for. All I wanted was to find out who killed Chrissy's daddy."

"The charges include attempted murder of a police officer and of a private citizen." Ray glowed. "She cooked her own goose. Even as one of the suspects, we had no concrete evidence against her until now."

"She might not have confessed if your questioning hadn't pushed her over the edge," said Lisa. "She was always aggressive, but I never thought she'd commit murder."

"I had no idea she was capable of this," Julie said. She squeezed Autumn's shoulder.

The police car drove off, Fran kicking the back seat, muffled screams heard as they drove past the gathering of friends.

ॐ

Vaughn Evans relaxed in first class. He thought about what he had left behind and what was ahead. His phone vibrated, a news item sent to his text alerts. The headline read *Fran Barnes Indicted for Murder*.

He opened the story to read it all, shocked that he had not seen it sooner, and disgusted that she named him as the cause of her killing spree. The story included his disappearance and role in the crime as Fran's big mouth gave the State evidence to confirm embezzlement on his part. Gary Martin's name was cleared. Vaughn's quick action in leaving the United States saved him from dealing with reporters and the law.

The thought of never returning to the United States made him realize the gravity of the situation, yet did not disturb him as much as he thought it would. His escape from Detective Reed bolstered Vaughn's ego. The plan for his new life complete with false identity, effectively erased him from the world.

ॐ

With Chrissy's case solved, Autumn threw a party to celebrate the emergence of a new life. The process of shedding doubt and anxiety continued, but lacked the darkness it contained before. The world seemed brighter and she felt supported. She opened to new possibilities and did not fear the future. To stay in the moment and embrace the present and those in her life with gratitude helped her overcome the tragedies of the past.

Stephanie Douglas, Julie Hall and her husband, Brad, Steve and Lisa Coleman, Maureen Roberts the realtor, and Ray Reed, along with all the pups, sat in Autumn's yard enjoying the late spring weather. White and red wines were open and a potluck lunch was set-up buffet style on the kitchen counter. Autumn thought Lisa's contribution was the best. It was great to hear about her progress since she had enrolled in culinary school with the vision of opening her own café. Lisa promised to have a dog-friendly outdoor eating area.

Stephanie watched Chrissy, Ace, Mickey, and Teddy playing in the grass, and considered getting one of her own. Autumn had already agreed to watch the new fur baby while Stephanie was at work if she got one.

Steve was off all painkillers and taking Tai Chi classes to enhance his balance.

Julie was on her second slice of strawberry shortcake. Autumn saw Julie savor every bite and wondered how she did not gain any weight despite her indulgences.

Maureen observed Autumn and Ray together and saw how happy they were. She hoped for the listing if she decided to sell her parents' house and purchase a new one.

The couple enjoyed their time with each other, along with friends. Ray wanted the next gathering to include some of his friends so they could meet Autumn. He was sure they would love her as much as he did.

Ray's angst over losing Vaughn, who summarily disappeared under an alias, prevented him from pursuing the case. The authorities felt it was not worth the time or expense to find him or discover his alias. The Lawyers' Fund for Client Protection reimbursed the stolen money to Vaughn's and Gary's clients. Ray was glad to inform Dean Sanders that he could come out of hiding from Vaughn. Dean's associates remained a threat, wanting their money.

Having sold Gary's house and paying the balance of the mortgage, Anna Martin suffered through the disappointment of her twenty-thousand dollar inheritance. She faced a tedious life of caretaking and scraping by.

Fran was spending three life sentences for premeditated murder in the State Correctional Institution in Muncy, Pennsylvania. A special pets-in-prison program allowed her to bring her cats with her after a psychiatrist confirmed that her explosive emotional state would somewhat stabilize as a result.

Chrissy's nightmares lessened with each passing week, the mutual love and affection with Autumn healed her grief and allowed her to move on while holding fond memories of her daddy.

Everything Autumn had experienced and survived had restored her faith. She no longer needed medication but continued sessions with Dr. Wes. The love of Chrissy and Ray kept her balanced and safe. Episodes of panic came farther apart. When it did happen, she had unconditional support that allowed continuous improvement. The memory of her parents' death was still painful, yet she remembered the good times more often and without the tears.

She recalled her mother's wisdom that love is the greatest healer of all, with a smile rather than anxiety. Ray and Chrissy helped her believe in love and its ability to heal. She knew that love lasts beyond death and that her parents were together watching over her. She felt that they approved of Ray.

The lesson was clear: there is no fear in truly loving, for it protects from the harshest of circumstances. Anxiety is fear, but love, faith, and hope are tonics to surmount whatever we must face.

~ ~ ~

Thanks for reading the first book in the Chrissy's Mysteries series. I hope you enjoyed it. If you liked getting to know Chrissy and Autumn, please leave a review on Amazon, Barnes & Noble, or Goodreads. If you want to know what happens next, you can purchase *The Dog-eared Diary*, book two in the series, at your favorite online bookstore. Read on for a special sneak preview of the first two chapters *of The Dog-eared Diary*!

You can also discover my other work and sign-up to my community for updates on the Chrissy's Mysteries series, special offers, and other works at www.DianeWingAuthor.com.

The Dog-eared Diary:

A Chrissy the Shih Tzu Mystery

Book Two

Sneak Preview!

Missing Person Report – Abigail Peabody– Knollwood, PA

Abigail Hempstead Peabody of Knollwood, PA was reported missing by her husband, Horatio Peabody, on August 7th, 1935. She is 5' 6" weighing 115 pounds, with dark hair and brown eyes. She was last seen by her husband at the West Chester train station on her way to visit relatives in New York who said she never arrived. Anyone with information regarding the whereabouts of Mrs. Peabody, contact the Knollwood police department immediately.

Obituary– Horatio Peabody (1878 – 1957) – Knollwood, PA

Wealthy local businessman, Horatio Peabody, died at home on July 13th, 1957 after a short hospitalization, surrounded by his family. He is survived by his son, Maynard, and daughter-in-law, Jillian Smith Peabody, and grandson, Edgar. He was a respected member of his community and donated 60 acres of land to Knollwood Township to be eternally preserved as a public park and recreation area. Services will be held at Sacred Blessing Presbyterian Church at 93 Main Street, July 20th, 1957.

≠1≠

The side of her fist slammed onto the polished desktop, moving the air toward Oxnard Peabody's face.

"You're keeping something from me, and I want to know what it is!"

"The secrets I keep are for your own good, Beatrice." Oxnard sighed. His sister tested his patience on a regular basis.

Beatrice folded her arms in a defiant stance.

They had been through all of this before. Oxnard knew she was hell-bent on changing everything in her favor. And discovering family secrets he promised his father he would keep. Oxnard dug his shiny black wingtips into the worn rug under his desk.

A sinister grin filled Beatrice's face. "I'm next in line to inherit the stone mansion."

"The house is not meant for you."

"Then for who?"

"Be happy with your trust fund and leave the rest to me."

"You don't even live there. Why not hand it over while you're still alive?"

"There is a reason I don't live there, Beatrice. Great-Grandfather Horatio left specific stipulations regarding the house."

"Now that it's yours, you could change that condition."

"His mouth turned down. "Don't you think I'd want to live in our family's legacy? And you along with me?"

"Aren't you afraid I'd kill you in your sleep?"

The thought had occurred to Oxnard many times when they lived under the same roof. From the day Beatrice appeared, his life changed and his stress increased. He struggled to hold his rolling executive chair in place the way he had held his fear around Beatrice. His deepest desire was to get far away from his sister's fury.

"I certainly hope not." Oxnard's voice was steady, but his pulse raced.

Beatrice let out a disbelieving growl. "What's the reason, then?"

"Father said the house was evil."

"Oh, come on, Oxnard. You don't really believe that, do you? There's no such thing!"

Oxnard saw Beatrice's dark brown eyes flash the way they used to just before she sucker-punched him in childhood and knew that, in fact, evil did exist.

"He told me to protect you."

"I don't need protection, but you do." Beatrice grimaced.

Oxnard shook his head, suddenly exhausted.

"How many times are we going to have this conversation? Let it go."

"Not likely."

Oxnard let out the breath he did not know he was holding.

"Don't negate the family history. Think about how unlucky Grandmother Abigail was in that house. She was ill before her disappearance. Great Grandfather Horatio suffered from alcoholism. Grandfather Maynard lived there until Grandmother Jillian had a miscarriage. She refused to live there after that. Once they moved, they were able to have Father. Mother and Father chose not to live there to avoid the dread that surrounds that building and the bad luck that follows. I signed over their house to you and bought one for myself. Isn't that enough?"

Beatrice ignored his generosity and challenged Oxnard. "I could make the Board of the Peabody Foundation decide."

"The Peabody Mansion is not part of the Foundation. It is mine. The Board has no say in this matter. They only have the right to distribute funds for its role in the community as a museum, not to determine ownership. This discussion is over." Oxnard's innards felt like mush. He was ready for Beatrice to leave.

"I disagree. There's a way around everything, and I'm going to find it."

"Let's just get through the day, shall we?" Oxnard wearied of this discussion and her presence.

A hard knock on the heavy wood paneled door disrupted the argument. Oxnard was thankful to whoever was on the other side of the door. Beatrice pressed her lips together in frustration.

"Come in!"

Greg Manning, the caretaker of Peabody Mansion and manager of the Peabody Festival, filled the doorway with his imposing muscular build and sandy blond hair. He had been a trusted member of the Peabody staff for the majority of his thirty-seven years, having come to them out of high school. Their father, Edgar, had hired him for the summer out of the need to care for the outside of the mansion. He'd never left, and Greg's duties expanded.

Beatrice glared at him. Oxnard noticed that Greg's wink and bright smile did nothing to melt the icy stare.

"Are you coming out soon? The place is getting mobbed and they're looking for the master of ceremonies to kick things off."

Oxnard did not enjoy public speaking and his argument with Beatrice did not put him in a social mood. This task would test his acting skills to the breaking point.

"Yes, as soon as we're finished our conversation."

"I think we're done," said Beatrice, "for now."

Beatrice stormed out of the office and slammed the door behind her.

Greg stared after her and then looked at Oxnard, who shrugged. Greg nodded in understanding. Oxnard recognized Greg's acceptance. He had experienced many fights between the siblings over the years. It was a way of life and a constant source of embarrassment for Oxnard.

"Give me a minute," said Oxnard.

"Okay, boss," said Greg as he quietly closed the door behind him.

Oxnard stayed in his chair, praying that she would not ruin the annual Peabody Festival in honor of Great Grandfather Horatio. A slight tremor moved through his body, as it did after each encounter with Beatrice. He wanted to love her, to take care of her, but she made it so very hard.

2

Autumn Clarke, her Shih Tzu, Chrissy, and best friend Stephanie Douglas walked through the late August heat shimmering over the annual Peabody Festival grounds. Packed with locals and visitors alike, the festival was an important part of Knollwood's economy. The town benefitted from the influx of tourists who filled the bed and breakfasts, restaurants, and Main Street retailers. The number of vendors and booths at the festival itself seemed to double over last year, with rows of tents added to the center of the fair grounds and an expanded stage area.

Autumn and Stephanie scanned the schedule of speeches and bands and map of vendor tables handed to them at the gate, intending to visit as many booths as possible before twilight fell. Once it got dark, the blasts from the fireworks display would upset Chrissy and make her whole body tremble. Autumn wanted to be home before that happened.

Autumn watched Chrissy's tail bounce up and down as her hips swayed side-to-side. Chrissy sniffed the freshly mowed grass and sneezed.

"Bless you, sweetheart," said Autumn.

Chrissy looked up at Autumn with a glistening nose, wagged her tail, and continued her joyful trot. Autumn watched her, proud that Chrissy had come such a long way in the three months since she'd lost her daddy and Autumn became her pet parent. Chrissy's resilience inspired Autumn to move past her own grief at the loss of her parents six months before.

The soaring heat did not seem to bother Chrissy, despite her long, silky hair. The warm breeze cut into the humidity and blew through Chrissy's bangs. If her precious Shih Tzu got thirsty, Autumn had the water bottle and portable cup at the ready.

They strolled past lines of eager patrons waiting in line to cool down at the water ice, lemonade, and ice cream stands. They had started at the row to the right of the entry gate, and were about a quarter of the way through, getting hungry as lunchtime approached. As if made to order, the bright yellow tent and bold flowing red font announced *Coleman's Kitchen*. Autumn and Stephanie smiled at each other and sped-up the pace. Lisa Coleman greeted them with a big smile and open arms.

"Ladies! Thanks for stopping by!"

"We wouldn't miss it!" said Autumn and Stephanie in unison as if they planned it. The two women had been best friends since they roomed together at Villanova and often finished each other's sentences.

Stephanie's enthusiasm about Lisa's cooking skills began after tasting her crab quiche at Autumn's house. It was nice to have a neighbor so accomplished in the culinary arts.

Autumn was proud of Lisa's decision to pursue a career she loved, especially after the awful experience she had at the law firm she worked for this past spring. She had a couple of years left in her culinary program at The Restaurant School in Philadelphia, but that did not stop her from opening her own restaurant in the meantime. She'd learned to cook from her mother, who passed away from cancer, and found that she was a natural chef. Lisa's father, Steve Coleman, supported his daughter's dream. He and Lisa lived a few doors down from Autumn and was pet parent to Chrissy's best friend, Mickey the standard poodle.

"How's business at the restaurant?" Autumn asked.

"Good. My biggest competition is Patsy's Deli, but my rotating menu keeps patrons tired of the same old lunch coming in. Patsy's makes breakfast, too, but I don't think I'll move into that. Maybe I'll start serving dinner or catering at some point, but with school, I just don't have the time to do anything but lunch."

They bit into the samples of Lisa's signature Mediterranean sandwich with lemon hummus, assorted veggies, and feta cheese on naan.

"Mmm," Autumn groaned, "this is so good."

Stephanie nodded, her mouth full.

Lisa beamed.

"Do you have a full-size version available?" Stephanie asked, looking around for a table. She spotted one at the corner of Lisa's tent.

"Yep. What do you want to drink?"

"Water's fine," said Autumn. "I'll take a Mediterranean sandwich, too, please."

Despite Lisa's insistence to the contrary, Autumn and Stephanie purchased their lunch. They were all for supporting their friend's enterprise. Lisa threw a couple of jumbo chocolate chip cookies on the tray as a bonus.

Enjoying the shade under the tent, Chrissy got her bowl of water and a grain-free snack and settled herself in the cool grass beneath the table. It was the perfect respite before continuing their exploration of the festival offerings. They perused the list of vendors and activities as they ate. A child ran by with his face painted like a tiger.

"I think we can skip the face-painting booth," said Stephanie with a chuckle.

"Agreed," said Autumn.

"Hi, Miss Douglas!" a little girl called from a nearby table.

Stephanie taught fifth grade at Knollwood Elementary school and often saw her students out and about.

"Hey, Cindy! Are you having fun?" Stephanie waved to Cindy's mother sitting next to the child. "Hi, Mrs. Tandy."

The woman waved, her mouth around a sandwich.

"You have Miss Jenkins for sixth grade, right?"

"Yeah," Cindy sounded disappointed.

"You're going to love her. She likes to have fun in her classroom. Plus, you're a great student, so you'll do great. "

Cindy brightened and then spotted Chrissy. "Can I pet your dog?"

"Sure, she loves the attention. Her name is Chrissy," Autumn said.

Cindy bent down and reached under the table. Chrissy came out to make it easy for the girl to reach her and wagged her tail.

"Hi, Chrissy. You're so soft! Your bow is so pretty."

Chrissy's topknot set-off by a pink satin flower clip was a kid pleaser every time. Cindy's touch was very gentle.

"Hey! She just smiled at me!"

Autumn did not doubt it. Chrissy had an expressive face.

"I'll see you in a couple of weeks, okay?" said Stephanie.

Cindy nodded, said goodbye to Chrissy, and went back to her lunch.

Brad Hall, another of Autumn's neighbors, walked by in his park ranger uniform, at the festival in an official capacity. He waved. Autumn knew his wife, Julie, was at the festival, too, operating the bake sale booth to raise money for school activities.

"Let's go find Julie," suggested Autumn. She moved her finger along the festival map. "Her booth is a few down from this one."

They didn't have to look hard, since Chrissy spotted her friend, Teddy the Yorkshire terrier before Autumn and Stephanie realized they had arrived at the booth. Julie was Teddy's pet parent. Chrissy pulled Autumn to where her friend stood, wagging his tail.

"Can I interest you in something to enjoy at home?" Julie smiled at them as she reached down to pet Chrissy. "How are you, little one?"

"I'm running low on snickerdoodles, so how about a small pack of those?" Stephanie dug in her purse for the money.

"I'll take a pack of chocolate chip cookies and that chocolate coconut Bundt cake."

Julie raised her eyebrows. "Buying for two, I take it?"

Autumn smiled. "As a matter of fact, yes. Ray has a sweet tooth."

"That's why he picked you, isn't it?" Julie laughed at her own joke. "You've gotten quite close over the last few months. You're the talk of the town."

"Well, investigating a murder is an intimate affair."

Together, they solved the murder of Chrissy's original pet parent. Ray and his German shepherd dog Ace saved Autumn and Chrissy from getting killed themselves. "It's not every day you find a great guy who is protective and understanding of my post-traumatic stress disorder.

It was six months since the fatal car accident that killed her parents and the start of her PTSD challenges. She still missed them, but Ray brought his healing love to her rescue, as did Chrissy.

"One day I hope to find someone who loves me as much as Ray loves Autumn.

"You will," said Autumn and squeezed Stephanie's arm.

Packages in hand, they said their goodbyes, planning to walk the fur babies together the following day. They stopped to play a few games, but did not win anything, laughing at each other's lack of accuracy at the ring toss and the shooting gallery. Halfway around the fairgrounds, they ran into Steve Coleman and Mickey. Chrissy's tail went into overdrive as she sniffed Mickey and hopped in greeting.

They walked past the hot dog stand, and Chrissy's and Mickey's noses lifted to take in the aroma of the fragrant meat. Autumn's friend, Maureen Roberts, a local realtor, was taking her turn at the realty booth, surrounded by books filled with photos of available properties. The festival drew out-of-towners looking to relocate or purchase a second home.

Maureen had been friends with Autumn's mother and offered to sell Autumn's house when she was ready. Autumn was not sure she would ever be ready to leave the house where she grew up. It held too many memories, which both helped and hurt her progress in therapy. The constant reminder that her parents were gone was difficult, yet the familiar environment provided some solace. Then again, if things kept moving in the right direction with Ray, it could be time to get a place they could call their own. Stella and George Clarke had left everything to Autumn, so she owned her house outright, but it would always feel like it was her house rather than Ray's and hers.

Screams came from the Round Up, a cylinder spinning so fast that riders were pinned to the wall. Autumn's group decided to stay on the ground. Feedback screeched from the loudspeakers, getting everyone's attention and forcing Chrissy to hide between Autumn's legs. Autumn lifted her under her little front legs and hugged her close. Chrissy's paws sat on Autumn's shoulders, her furry head snuggled against her face. Autumn kissed her silky ear.

"It's okay," she whispered to Chrissy and then to her friends, "She'll be okay in a minute."

"Attention everyone! Our host, Oxnard Peabody, is about to take the stage."

Another screech of feedback exacerbated Chrissy's trembling. Her usually soft-smelling fur took on a mild pungent odor of fear. Autumn held her close and supported her head against her shoulder, bouncing her like a baby.

Autumn tried to distract her. "Look at Mickey! What's he doing?" but Chrissy only cuddled closer, so she resorted to making kissy sounds on her ear.

"Let's walk toward the stage. She'll calm down," Autumn said.

The group made their way across the grassy midway. Smells of popcorn, hot dogs, and cotton candy wafted on the air. The walking motion seemed to lull Chrissy, and the scented air caught her attention. Autumn felt her relax.

"Ready to walk?"

Chrissy lifted her head from Autumn's shoulder and made a grunting sound. Autumn placed Chrissy on the ground. She shook her luxurious white and gray coat and took her place beside Mickey, who nuzzled her. Autumn, impressed by Chrissy's ability to regain her emotional balance, considered her a good example for her own recovery.

People stood behind the already filled folding chairs. Greg Manning took the stage and tapped the microphone. Autumn checked on Chrissy, but the noise left her unfazed.

"Welcome to the eightieth Peabody Festival, celebrating Horatio Peabody and his generous donation of sixty acres of land to our community. Generations of Knollwood residents have enjoyed his legacy, and each year, our beautiful community draws thousands of visitors to Knollwood. We are glad to share this day with residents and visitors alike. Now, I'm honored to introduce Horatio's great-grandson, Oxnard Peabody."

The crowd applauded, with locals whistling and yelling Oxnard's name. The residents appreciated the Peabody family's generosity over the years and the festival was the most anticipated event for its fun and historical significance.

"Greg gets better looking each time I see him," said Stephanie.

"Have you ever met him?" Autumn asked.

"No, but I wouldn't mind."

"Let's see if we can bump into him before the day is over." She felt a mischievous smile adorn her lips.

171

Stephanie nodded as she clapped for Oxnard, who was encouraging quiet.

"Each year, the Peabody Festival expands to include more visitors and wonderful businesses. My great-grandfather Horatio would have been pleased to see how the celebration has grown and how much happiness his contribution to the community has brought to Knollwood. Thousands of feet have walked upon this ground to pay tribute to Horatio Peabody and his dedication to the community. We thank you for that.

"This year, there is a special surprise that very few people know about. I, Oxnard Peabody, am the featured victim at the dunking booth, wearing everything except my shoes. For the next several hours, you'll get to try your skill and see if you can soak me as I sacrifice myself for the cause. All proceeds from the dunking booth will go to the care and maintenance of Peabody Park and the Peabody Mansion Museum. We appreciate your support!"

Oxnard exited the stage to wild applause and laughter at the thought of this staid icon of the community being soaked, fully clothed, in the dunking tank. People started moving to get in line to try their hand at toppling him from his perch.

"I don't plan to participate in the dunking. There's no joy in seeing someone fall into water, plus I have lousy throwing skills," said Stephanie.

"I saw Greg walk over near the tent housing Jade's Jewelry. We can do a little shopping and see if you can get his attention."

Stephanie sucked in her lips, nervous about talking to Greg, and gave Autumn a big-eyed stare.

"What's the worst that can happen?" Autumn asked, and started walking toward the tent.

"I guess I could use some new jewelry."

"I'm heading to the hot dog stand. Mickey's been interested since we got here. I wouldn't mind one myself. We'll catch-up with you." Steve and Mickey headed toward the tantalizing smell of the hot dog vendor.

Autumn, Chrissy, and Stephanie made their way to the jewelry booth. Jade's had some of the best costume and natural stone jewelry and accessories in the area. The booth sparkled with necklaces, rings, earrings, beaded bags, and bracelets. The women worked their way around the U-shaped table arrangement to make sure they did not miss anything.

They held up various pieces to see if they flattered and gave honest opinions to one another about the look. Autumn went for the earthier pieces, with opaque natural stones and fresh water pearls attracting her attention. Stephanie liked bling; if it sparkled, it caught her eye.

Autumn spotted some rhinestone hairclips that looked perfect for Chrissy. The furry diva sat still while her mommy held up several designs for her. Autumn put four of them in her mini-shopping basket; two matching pink rhinestone clips for pigtails and one each of yellow and clear rhinestones for topknots.

"You'll look so pretty."

Chrissy looked at her and smiled.

"I don't see Greg," said Stephanie, as they made their way to the back of the tent.

"Shhh, listen."

There were two male voices, angry but restrained, their growls muffled by the canvas curtains at the back of the tent.

"You can't be serious!"

"I've smelled it on you before and let it go, but being drunk at an important event is unacceptable. You're finished."

"But, I..."

Footsteps stomped away. Autumn looked down and saw Chrissy with her head halfway under the canvas looking at the commotion.

"Chrissy, come here sweetie."

She pulled her head from under the curtain and sat next to Autumn, who crouched down beside her. She whispered in Chrissy's ear.

"What did you see? Show Mommy."

A wave of nausea came over Autumn and a vision of wing-tip shoes walking away. The image faded.

"One of the men was Oxnard," she said to Stephanie.

"How do you know that?"

"I recognized the voice." Autumn felt bad lying to Stephanie. Even though Stephanie was her best friend and trustworthy, Chrissy's ability was an odd and unlikely gift that Autumn preferred not to share. Maybe at some point in the future, but not yet. She was still coming to grips with it herself. Ray was the only other person who knew Chrissy's secret, out of necessity to solve the last case.

"What about the other one?"

"We saw Greg come this way, so it could have been him. I don't see him around."

Autumn heard the disappointment in Stephanie's voice.

"You may have just dodged a bullet. If he's an alcoholic, you don't want to date him no matter how handsome he is."

"True, but we still don't know if it was Greg. I'd rather give him the benefit of the doubt." Stephanie sighed and put a shimmering necklace in her basket.

They checked out and kept walking. Nearby, the sound of splashing and laughter rose above the din.

"Someone must have nailed the target and dunked Oxnard. Maybe it will cool him off."

"I hope so. I teach my students that holding onto anger hurts your heart."

A few booths down, Barbara McCarthy, owner of Attic Treasures Books, stood behind stacks of antiquarian and used books. Early on in their relationship, Autumn and Stephanie bonded over their love of books. They spent hours combing through library sales and used bookshops. Barbara had an extensive collection of out-of-print and hard-to-find volumes. She was also the town historian. The women knew Barbara from their visits to her shop, as most locals did.

"Looking for anything in particular?"

"I'll know it when I see it," said Stephanie, already absorbed in the hunt.

"Me, too. We may be here for a while."

"Can this little girl have a snack?"

Chrissy was on a grain-free diet, including snacks, but Autumn did not like turning away kindhearted folks who wanted to give her a treat. Chrissy usually made the right decision to eat it or not.

"Sure."

Autumn watched Chrissy politely take the small bone-shaped cookie, hold it in her mouth while Barbara watched, and placed it on the ground as soon as soon as she turned away.

Having found a few choice volumes, they headed across the field looking for Steve and Mickey. Autumn scanned the area. In the center of the open field, Chrissy stopped cold. Autumn gently tugged her leash to get her moving, but she would not budge. Chrissy barked until Autumn looked down and then began digging.

"What are you doing?" Autumn asked.

Chrissy's head stayed down, her claws rapidly displacing grass and dirt. No amount of encouragement coaxed her away from the spot. Several minutes later, Stephanie gasped. A bony finger poked out of the ground, accusing an unknown perpetrator. Chrissy sat next to her discovery, panting.

Autumn whipped out her cell phone and dialed Ray. Stephanie went to find Brad Hall, the park ranger.

About the Author

Diane is the author of seven books, an avid reader, bibliophile, lover of trees and animals, and a lifelong learner. She and her husband are pet parents to a sweet little Shih Tzu named Chrissy. Check out her books and sign-up for the latest news about Diane's work at DianeWingAuthor.com.

In this second installment in the series, Chrissy digs up clues to help Autumn solve a historical disappearance and a modern-day murder mystery

Autumn Clarke is getting her life back to normal with the help of her extraordinary shih tzu, Chrissy, when the death of a local philanthropist reveals the man's dark family secrets, as well as unexpected ties to Autumn. When Chrissy discovers a dog-eared diary in the dead man's family home, Autumn discovers that things in the Clarke family are not quite as they seem. Can Autumn interpret the hidden clues in the dog-eared diary to crack the most puzzling disappearance in Knollwood history? Are the recent murders connected to the past? Is Chrissy more insightful than Autumn realized?

"I have fallen in love with Chrissy and Autumn and their continuing journey to health while finding themselves in the middle of a murder mystery adventure. My pre-teen daughter and I enjoyed reading *The Dog-Eared Diary* and then discussing the clues, plot twists, and characters."
—Antoinette Brickhaus, Maryland

"Chrissy the Shih Tzu is a real character in the book and not just a prop to help the story along. Chrissy often felt like she was going to start talking. I loved the relationship between Autumn and her dog. The love the two of them have is absolutely perfect. Perfect for a rainy afternoon and one any cozy mystery fan will enjoy. I can't wait to see what happens next!"
—Andrea J. Guy

"I applaud the author for her use of so many clever writing devices within a rather brief cozy mystery. Nothing seemed contrived nor out-of-place. I hope that someone makes the decision to adapt these books to the screen because it would make one amazing mystery series!"
—Ruth A. Hill, journalist

Learn more at www.DianeWingAuthor.com

From Modern History Press

Prepare to be tricked & treated in this third installment of the Chrissy the Shih Tzu cozy mysteries!

Fall has arrived in Knollwood, and Autumn Clarke is planning an elaborate Halloween event at The Peabody Mansion B&B to support the local animal shelter. With the entire town invited and the inn not officially open for overnight guests, an unexpected request lands Dana Wood, an A-list actor, as a long-term guest while shooting her latest movie in New Hope. Autumn and the gang step in to help with her baggage filled with betrayal, scandal, unsolved murder, a personal secret, and a cast of eccentric, suspicious characters. As the filming begins, Chrissy's shrewd judge of character and nose for unearthing incriminating evidence provide the backdrop for this twisty and thrilling tale.

Bonus features: book club questions, recipes of meals from the book, and a Halloween scavenger hunt list appear at the end of the book!

"Autumn and Chrissy have become my favorite crime solvers!! Diane Wing has put together another fun rainy afternoon, cuddle-with-my-dog in-a-corner-window mystery! Throughout this series we have seen Autumn and Chrissy overcome tragedy, find love, and solve some murders! All her supporting characters make sense and are loveable. A great read for anyone from 8 to 80!!"

-- Antoinette B., Leonardtown, MD

"I loved how the plot unfolded and how I was kept in suspense about the killer's identity until the end. ...a delightful, fast-paced and engaging book well worth reading. It is a great standalone book, even if you haven't read the first two."

-- Terri Chalmers, Sicklerville, NJ

Learn more at www.DianeWingAuthor.com

From Modern HIstory Press www.ModernHistoryPress.com

www.ingramcontent.com/pod-product-compliance
Lightning Source LLC
Chambersburg PA
CBHW051138020726
47501CB00005B/1570